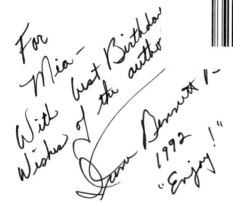

For
Mia —
With best Birthday
Wishes of the author

Gene Bennett —
1992
"Enjoy!"

Morning Glory
Afternoon

Morning Glory Afternoon

by
Irene Bennett Brown

Blue Heron Publishing, Inc.
Hillsboro, Oregon

PUBLISHER'S CATALOGING IN PUBLICATION DATA

Brown, Irene Bennett.
Morning glory afternoon.

SUMMARY: In 1924 a 17-year-old girl tries to rebuild her life after a personal tragedy by taking a job as switchboard operator in a small town far from home. Instead of a haven, however, she finds her new community in the grip of fanatic prejudices that force her to take a stand for what she knows is right.
[1. Prejudices—Fiction. 2. Ku Klux Klan (1915–)
—Fiction. 3. Conduct of life—Fiction] I. Title.
PZ7.B81387Mo   [Fic]   91-072118
ISBN 0-936085-20-7

Published by
Blue Heron Publishing, Inc.
24450 N.W. Hansen Road
Hillsboro, Oregon 97124
503.621.3911

First Sunflower Editions Printing October 1991
Library of Congress Catalog Card Number: 91-072118

❁

for my husband
Bob
with gratitude and love

❁

Chapter 1

JESSAMYN FABER was the last incoming passenger to step from the train that summer afternoon of 1924. She fumbled forward a few steps, then halted, feeling very alone, bewildered.

A strange voice barked at her, "You're in the way, Miss! Step aside."

"S-sorry." The hot fuely air was hard to breathe. Further away, Jessy set her heavy embroidered satchel down by her silk-stockinged ankles. This was so far—from home.

Ought she to've stayed there? On The Ranch, two hundred miles behind her now to the east? In spite of…? Jessy trembled. No. She was right to leave. It was time she got some starch in her backbone. She had to stop being a scared child. She was seventeen. Nearly a grown woman.

She tucked a damp curl behind her ear, made right the comb-fastened swirl of auburn hair on the back of her head, and blinked back the tears in her eyes. She was here. Ardensville, Kansas. She could see it painted on the high water tank opposite the glittering tracks. Drawing a deep breath, she picked up her satchel and began to walk.

She'd known that Ardensville was a windy sun-baked town near the Colorado border. But nobody had told her it was a pretty town. The ache in her throat lessened. She especially liked the trees. Elm and cottonwoods lined the brick street; the street itself was so clean it looked washed. Well-kept yards. Houses with shades drawn against the sun were like islands of peacefulness.

She wondered if Mama and Papa were feeling better, too, about her coming to Ardensville. They'd been so worried for her. In her mind, Jessy heard again her sister Willow's voice, helping to persuade Mama and Papa:

"Let Jessy go. Give her a chance to forget, six months or a year away from here, she might be able to. We ought to help Jessamyn any way we can, to make her understand once and for all that that boy's—Farley Baxter's accident—wasn't her doing."

Farley. Jessy shivered in the brassy sunshine. No matter what anybody said, she was to blame. Not that she could explain everything yet. But it was her fault. The dark feeling threatened again, now, and Jessy set her jaw to block the pain.

In spite of wanting not to, she recalled how bad school had been from late winter through graduation. After that, on the farm, she had found many ways to keep her hands busy, but not her mind. Over and over again she would see ice, black water, the last moments of terror on Farley's face. Jessy's mouth dried, remembering.

At the top of summer their neighbor, Auberta Steele, brought news that for Jessy was a light at the end of a tunnel. A distant cousin named Mrs. Augusta "Gussie" Stuberg, Auberta told them, owned a small, independent telephone company in western Kansas. She was looking to hire a telephone operator—a dependable "hello girl," a dedicated "central." Wouldn't it help young Jessamyn to get away? Live a different life for a while, in a new town? Would she want the job?

Did she? Oh, desperately! Though Mama and Papa had had doubts to the end. But she was here. Truly here in Ardensville for an interview with Mrs. Stuberg, and a trial work period as switchboard operator.

Jessy saw that even Ardensville's livery stable was tidy, and next door to it, the blacksmith shop.

She passed a lot crowded with giant red tractors, shiny silver discs, mowers and rakes. This implement yard would be like heaven to Papa, who still farmed with horses. LOMBARD A. HALE, PROPRIETOR, the sign over the yard gate said.

Further on, an automobile agency also seemed to be owned by Lombard A. Hale. Jessy looked with interest at the dazzling automobiles inside the large glass-fronted building. Fancy autos were rare back home in Seena, though more and more folks were buying themselves a car. She felt a tingle of excitement, walking on. In all her life she'd never lived in a town before.

Jessamyn changed the satchel to her other hand. Each place of business, Burmann's Department Store, Pierce's Pharmaceutical, a barber shop, grocery store, a beauty shop and movie theater—looked prosperous. She couldn't see many customers, though, this lazy, hot afternoon.

No wonder. Taking a tiny handkerchief from under the navy cuff that edged her white puff sleeve, Jessy dabbed her perspiring face. Two eating places on this street, she noticed, as well as Grant's Emporium way down there. She wasn't hungry. But she'd dearly like to put the satchel down a spell. The heat was too much.

It was Willow, two years older than she, who often said, "Jessamyn is like a morning glory flower. Let the sun come out hot, and Jessy's pretty face goes into hiding." True enough, she supposed. The younger kids in the family would say so, too. Jessy shaded her eyes with her free hand and read, MANDY'S, on the window of the smaller cafe. It would do.

As Jessy slipped onto a stool at the counter, a pleasant-faced rather heavy-set girl came forward, eyeing Jessy closely. She smiled, "I'm Mandy. New in town? What can I get you?"

Jessy gave a quick nod, a brief smile. "My name is Jessy Faber. I'm trying for a job here as telephone operator. Would you—" she hesitated—"bring me a glass of cold milk—and a doughnut, please?" Mandy bustled away.

Eating, since the bad time with Farley, was troublesome more often than not, but it felt good to be sitting down. Jessamyn's feet, aching in their unaccustomed patent pumps, rested atop the satchel. She couldn't sit long, though. The afternoon would be gone too soon. She looked worriedly at the clock on the wall. Before dark she *had* to be in a room somewhere, settled.

With persistence, the milk and the doughnut disappeared to the last sip and crumb. Jessy hefted her satchel and stumbled toward the cafe door as two ranchers entered. One, the younger cowboy, brown-skinned and with eyes as blue as mountain lakes, grinned shyly. He stepped back out onto the sidewalk and held the door open for Jessy. As he tipped his hat, the sun dazzled off a small ornament that decorated his carved leather hatband. She gave him a smile of thanks and considered asking him, or Mandy, for directions to Mrs. Augusta Stuberg's house. No, she would find Third and Elm street without help. From now on she had to count on herself.

A quarter of an hour later Jessy located the house. A board sidewalk led to the small cottage set back from the side street. On a screen-enclosed porch Jessy could see a dumpy-looking woman surrounded by a jungle of overgrown houseplants, rocking in a green slatted swing. Canaries in several cages were singing.

Jessy started to knock at the screen door but hesitated, unsure what she ought to do as the woman began to talk with great feeling to no one Jessy could make out. "…takes every widowman for herself… nobody else a chance….” The canaries sang insanely through it all.

Drawing a long breath, Jessamyn said very loud, “M-Mrs. Stuberg?”

There was an abrupt silence from the woman, though the birds sang on. Jessy chewed her lip and waited. The satchel was so heavy she couldn’t hold onto it any longer. She let it thump to the boardwalk.

“What was that?” The woman inside croaked. She leaped to her feet and bustled over to peer at Jessy through the locked screen door. “Who are you? I’ve got the fidgets bad enough th’out having the living daylights scared out’ve me besides!”

“I-I’m truly sorry, I didn’t mean to—” *She was off to a bad start already.* Jessy tried to smile. “My name is Jessamyn Faber. I wrote to you about the—the telephone operation p-position. I’m from—Seena? Eastern Kansas…?”

“Well, my yes! You’re the girl my cousin Auberta was sending to me. Wait a minute.” Mrs. Stuberg unhooked the screen door. She opened it wide. “You come in now, outta the heat. Let’s look at you. Skinny, ain’t you? White around the mouth—you sickly? Hope not. You’re mighty pretty. But pretty don’t make a good worker. Well, we’ll talk about it.”

Jessy picked up her bag and followed the woman inside where it was a trifle cooler. “Sit right—” Mrs. Stuberg started to say. She darted a guilty look at Jessamyn, then rushed to the swing where she shoved a flat, copper-colored bottle under the flowered cushion. Jessy started, wondering a bit.

“Sit down here with me?” It was a hesitant question.

Too weary to care about the woman’s odd actions, Jessy hauled the satchel to the swing and sank down with a grateful sigh. Almost immediately her nose picked up a faint, bitter odor. In spite of trying not to, Jessy’s nose twitched. She glanced at Mrs. Stuberg. The woman eyed her in defiance, almost.

Suddenly, Augusta Stuberg burped, making both of them jump. "Par'me, par'me," Mrs. Stuberg begged; "I didn't go to do that. My goodness." She continued to eye Jessy with something like suspicion and worry.

Jessy made herself settle back, although her heart beat furiously. The bottle she'd seen Mrs. Stuberg slip under the cushion was *bootleg whiskey.* She was a numbskull not to guess right away, the woman she was to work for, work with, was a whiskey drinker. Mama and Papa, if they had suspected such a thing, wouldn't have let her set foot off the farm. Panicky inside, Jessy nevertheless tried to smile in Gussie Stuberg's direction.

"I haven't had switchboard training, Mrs. Stuberg, but I'll work hard to learn. You won't be sorry you sent for me." She felt better, having said that much.

Augusta Stuberg nodded; the bulgy eyes glowed with relief. "Fine," she told Jessy. "I'll teach you. We'll get along." With a swift kick of her slippered foot, she set the swing in motion. "Don't let this go to your head, but you come high recommended by my cousin, Auberta Steele. Haven't seen the old girl in years, but we keep in touch. Tryin' to stay in each other's good graces now and then askin' the other a favor." She snorted. "Each of us hopin' the other will kick off first so we can inherit, me her farm, her my telephone company." She giggled as though it was a fine game.

"I owe thanks to Miss Steele," Jessy murmured. As difficult a neighbor as Auberta was to them sometimes, she'd known somehow that Jessy needed to get away and had thought of asking her cousin for this favor. With a start, Jessy realized that Gussie Stuberg had asked her a question. "Hmmm? I beg your pardon. What did you say?"

The look of annoyance on the toady face vanished. "I said, can you imagine, even in this modern day and age, nineteen twenty-four, some folks don't want their daughters leaving home till the day they marry? Don't want them *working out* even though they make good wages, five, ten dollars a week! They think they'll be in danger, come to some terrible end." Mrs. Stuberg stopped the swing. "Makes it hard for me, I tell you. Even in a town this size, I have trouble gettin' good help. Then when I do get a girl to work, she up and marries. Like Ruthie, the girl I got workin' the switchboard today. Gettin' married. You'll be replacin' her."

"I won't be getting marri—" Jessy tried to tell her.

Gussie, after a quick gulp of air, rushed on, "Pretty girls don't like to work weekends, either—"

Jessy wanted to tell her that keeping busy all the time was what she wanted more than anything, but still Mrs. Stuberg didn't give her a chance to speak.

"—supper here with me," Gussie Stuberg was saying, "when it cools down we'll walk downtown, and I'll show you the switchboard, the office. You'll live with me—"

"No!" Jessy cried, breaking in successfully this time. "I—I mean, thank you very much. But I really have to—I want to be— by myself." She clasped her hands tight in her lap and tried again, "I wouldn't be good company. Honestly, I wouldn't. There are things I have to settle, feelings to solve. It really would be best if I lived alone. You don't mind, do you, Mrs. Stuberg? Please, isn't there someplace where I can rent a room downtown?"

The woman studied Jessamyn's face. "You got a kinda' hurt look back in them eyes," she said. "What was it, a lover's quarrel?" She gave Jessy's hand a pat. "What happened?" When Jessy didn't answer right away, a mixed expression of anger and disbelief flickered across her face. "That selfish Auberta didn't write one word 'a this in her letters. What's it all about, honey?"

Jessy twitched uncomfortably. "I—I can't tell you; I don't want to talk about it. Please? I am sorry."

Gussie Stuberg's head bobbed. "Another time, you want to get it all off your chest, you come to me. I like gos—, I mean, I'm a good listener." She mumbled low, and Jessy could hardly hear her,

"Nobody ever wants to stay with me. There is that room back of the telephone office. Goes with the job free—"

"Yes," Jessy blurted, "I'd like a room at the telephone office. I'll be handy to work."

Gussie didn't seem to have heard. "Other'n that, there is Lilli Miller's boarding house, but that girl charges an arm and a leg, I bet, for her fancy rooms."

"Honest," Jessy implored, "the room at the telephone office will do. I'm sure it will." She nudged her satchel with a toe. "All I own is right there, my books, clothes; I won't need much space."

"But you will have your supper with me today?" The woman looked pathetically hopeful.

One refusal of her new boss' hospitality was enough. "Sure." Jessamyn smiled warmly. "I'd love to. Thank you."

It was terrible; the meat loaf, mashed potatoes and gravy, and applesauce all had a similar garbagey taste. A good cook herself from the time she was a little girl, Jessy recognized that fresher fixings would have helped Mrs. Stuberg's cooking. "Delicious," she said, nearly strangling as she swallowed, "very good." She hoped she wouldn't get sick.

The supper finally ended, Jessy hid her relief and helped Mrs. Stuberg clear the table.

Early evening fireflies hung in the warm, still air as they set out for downtown. Rested, anxious to see the telephone office and her room, Jessy now carried the satchel as though it were empty.

Chapter 2

JESSY SAW, from Augusta Stuberg's snaillike pace, that the woman wanted her company as long as possible. She good naturedly slowed down, nodding and exclaiming as Mrs. Stuberg told her about the town and some of its people.

"That," Gussie Stuberg said with a sniff, pointing to a stately Victorian house on the opposite side of the tree-lined street, "is the boarding house I was telling you about. Lilli Miller's. Girl ain't more'n twenty years old. Inherited that big house from her Aunt Martha Miller. Martha's only kin, this Lilli from St. Louis." She lowered her voice, "The girl has a *past*, if I don't miss my guess."

It didn't seem fair to judge Lilli Miller, not there to defend herself, so Jessy tried to change the subject. "It's a beautiful house. Ardensville has the prettiest houses and yards I've ever seen."

"Cecil Kinglake does the yards." Augusta looked pleased to tell her. "He's the town handyman and gardener. Does maintenance for the telephone company, too." She tapped the side of her head and gave Jessy a knowing look. "He's simple in the head. But he's likable, a nice boy who wouldn't hurt a fly."

"I—I'd like to meet him," Jessy said.

Gussie motioned with her head toward the restaurant where earlier Jessy had eaten a doughnut and milk. "The cafe over there is run by Mandy Phillips. Plain girl. Can't get a husband. Has to support herself."

"I liked her. I thought she was very nice. I planned to take my meals there—"

"—tell you who is nice," Mrs. Stuberg snatched the conversation back. "Lombard Hale is who. Whole town loves him. He's mayor here."

Remembering the name, Jessy put in, "He owns the farm implement yard, doesn't he, and the automobile agency?"

"Oh, that ain't all. Town was named for Lombard's mama's folk. She was an Arden. Mr. Hale is a pillar, that's what, a *pillar*." She gave a sigh. "A widower, too; handsome as all get out." A few steps farther along, Gussie Stuberg began to frown. "Here we are," she grunted.

The telephone office was a cubbyhole sandwiched between the drug store and the movie house, Jessy saw. On her earlier trip down Main Street, she hadn't noticed, but there it was—painted in gold letters on the plate glass front: ARDENSVILLE TELE-PHONE COMPANY.

Inside, a blonde girl sat on a stool in front of a cabinet-sized switchboard. She might have been a mannequin in a store window, or a fish in a bowl. That would be her in there soon. Jessy drew a shaky breath.

Spotting Mrs. Stuberg, the girl inside waved. Augusta Stuberg opened the door and pulled Jessy into the office. She put her satchel down. Trancelike, she went to look at the switchboard.

It made her think of an oaken kitchen cupboard, except with rows of metal-rimmed holes where doors might have been. Plugged into some of the holes were a web of crisscrossed cords coming from a tablelike affair in front of the girl. Higher, above the holes, were row upon row of little metal flaps. It looked awfully complicated! Jessy gave the operator, Ruthie, a wobbly smile.

"This here is Jessamyn Faber, our new operator from over Seena way, Ruthie," Gussie Stuberg said. "You can go home now, get on with your weddin' plans. I'll show Miss Faber the ropes tonight. She'll be ready then to take over in the morning."

Jessy was dismayed. "Tonight? But I—I...." She looked at Mrs. Stuberg, but the woman didn't seem to see her worry.

"Thanks, Mrs. Stuberg," Ruthie said. She smiled at Jessamyn. "It ain't hard at all. You'll catch on in no time."

What if she didn't? Jessy watched closely as a little metal flap dropped at the top of the board. In response, Ruthie yanked a pair of plug-ended cords down from the board. The dropped flap had been some kind of signal, Jessy guessed, watching as the cords flopped back into line. Ruthie reached over and put the metal flap back up. She pointed to a scribbled note tacked with others on a bulletin board beside the switchboard, near a clock. "Doc's out of town," she explained, "so it's no use to try to get him for a couple days."

Ruthie climbed off the stool and removed her headset. Gussie motioned for Jessy to take the stool. Managing what she hoped was a look of calm, Jessy sat down. "Show—show me what to do, pl-please."

Like a child being fitted for a costume, Jessamyn sat still and let Augusta settle the headset over her auburn hair. A mouthpiece curved up like a horn from a metal plate that rested on her chest. Jessy swallowed. Mrs. Stuberg adjusted the mouthpiece closer to Jessy's lips. She made sure the earphone rested properly over her right ear. The apparatus felt strange and cumbersome, but Jessy didn't comment when Mrs. Stuberg announced, "Now we're in business!"

Her boss pointed to the switchboard where a metal flap had dropped, and at the same time she pulled up a back cord. "Take this connection," she put it in Jessy's hand. "See that little bitty number thirty-six by the metal drop? All right. Plug the cord into the hole down here lower on the board that's marked thirty-six. Means somebody on thirty-six line wants to make a call." Jessy plugged in the cord. "Say 'Number please?,' but it's seven o'clock so that means it's old Hannah Lewelling callin' her sister."

Jessy's throat felt dry as burned toast. "N-number, please?" She sounded like a little child! Miraculously, from far away, a voice came back to her through the earphone. But, what were they saying? The voice sounded like rattling marbles. Jessy stammered, "I—I beg your pardon? What number did you want?"

Now the voice came sharp and clear, "Central! You know I want to talk to Marvella. It's seven o'clock. What's the matter with you?"

In panic, Jessy looked to Mrs. Stuberg for help.

"Right there," her boss hissed, "plug the *front* cord from that pair into number six line. Now push this here little key, this button—two long rings, one short."

With sweating fingers, Jessy did as she was told.

"Now then, was that so hard?" Mrs. Stuberg was actually laughing at her, Jessy realized, feeling foolish. Her boss reached up and pushed the metal flap back into place. "Leave the cords plugged in now so them old women can have their talk. It'll be a while. You'll know they're finished when Hannah rings back. The little flap will drop again, showing you they're through talking. Then you pull the cords out and put the flap up."

Jessy nodded to show she understood. "Th-that's all?" She sank back, pleased.

"Lordy," Mrs. Stuberg chuckled, "you ain't done. There's a drop," she pointed, "an' there's another. Get that one first. That's probably Mrs. Pierce wanting to call Mr. Pierce at his drugstore, to tell him his supper is hot and waiting. That other one is *them Bakers*! Wanting to know the time. Don't have a clock in the house, by the way they're always pestering Central, asking."

Jessy drew herself up again, wailing softly. "Ohhh—goodness! All—all right." Perspiring from the warm night and her jangled nerves, Jessy managed to connect Mrs. Pierce at home with Mr. Pierce at his drugstore, following Mrs. Stuberg's directions.

She took the other call. "N-number, please?" She darted a look at the clock on the wall, to the right of the board. "It is—six minutes after seven. Seven oh six." She'd give anything for a drink of water. *Relax for pity sake*, Jessy pleaded silently with herself.

With each call, the work became gradually easier. She began to watch for the flaps to drop, taking the calls on her own although Mrs. Stuberg stood at her elbow giving advice when needed. She handed Jessy a card on which was listed the names of all the telephone subscribers, their lines and rings. Jessy determined to memorize the list as soon as she could.

"You've caught on, you're doing fine," Mrs. Stuberg said after a while. "I'm going back to check your room, make sure Ruthie washed and dried the bedding before she put it back on, like I told her to. Eight o'clock, or thereabouts, you come on back. Ardensville folks go to bed with the chickens. Wouldn't be many nighttime calls so we don't give night service. Except in an emergency. They'll come knockin' on the door to wake you."

Time stretched longer and longer between clicking "drops." Jessy waited until eight-twenty, but by then the board was long since still. She'd gotten through her first stint as a working girl! A bit clumsy, maybe, but not so bad, either. Heaving a weary sigh, she took off the headset, unplugged it and let it lay on the board, then took up the satchel and went to look at her room.

It was smaller than she had pictured; badly in need of fresh paint and fresh air. It contained simply a rumpled cot, a chair, and a broken-down dresser. Her heart dipped. Afraid her boss would see how she felt, though, and try again to get her to come live with her, Jessy said, "Nice. The room will do fine."

Augusta opened a creaking door into a tinier room. "Got running water in here," she announced. She pointed to a moldy-looking sink and ancient bathtub. "Privy is in back, outside."

A while later, Augusta said good-bye, and Jessy was alone. It was different—so quiet. Not like being in the midst of the happy, noisy family at home. Closer inspection revealed that while the room might not be pleasant to look at, Ruthie had left it clean. Jessy unpacked, placing neat piles of folded clothing in the dresser drawer, and hanging her dresses on the rack provided at one end of the combination bath-dressing room.

Near the bottom of her satchel, Jessy's fingers came upon a small object. Her eyes filmed over as she looked at the tiny gold compact in the palm of her hand. Farley had given it to her the Christmas she was twelve. She shouldn't have brought it. But neither could she have left it behind. Like her memories, it was part of her.

Jessamyn put the compact away and undressed for bed. She pulled an airy light nightgown down over her head, let down her hair, and brushed it until it floated in deep coppery waves on her shoulders. She was so tired. Surely she would sleep tonight. She crawled onto the cot and lay back, drawing just the sheet over her in the warm room.

For a few hours, Jessy slept. Then sounds unfamiliar, town dogs barking, a train, woke her in the middle of the night. Awake, she began to remember, again. Last winter. Home.

SHE RAN WITH little slip-sliding steps around the iced-over picnic grove pond, laughing, "You can't catch me, Farley Baxter, you can't." She giggled and darted away from him. "And I won't say I love you. You can't make me."

"Don't tease, Jess. Say it. Be my steady girl. I'll die if you won't. Honest, do you love me, Jess?"

She looked back at him and laughed again as Farley struggled to keep his feet on the slippery ice. To tease him further she silently mouthed the three words, "I love you."

"Wh—? What did you say? Did you say it, Jessy, really? You did, Jessamyn Faber! Say you love me *loud*, so I can hear it, so the whole country will know. C'mon, Jess, please?"

She slid to a halt, cupped her mittened hands around her mouth and shouted, "I LOVE YOU, FARLEY BAXTER!" The second the words were out, Jessy wanted them back. She was ashamed. It wasn't true. She cared a lot, yes, she'd liked Farley for a long time, but not the way he meant. Her feeling of fun, her laughter, faded. She started toward Farley to apologize and explain.

Sounds, like soft, muffled rifle shots popped around her, grew louder. Jessy hesitated. Looking down she saw the ice separate under her feet. Crying out, she lurched toward firmer ice. Too late. Jessy knew a gradual stinging pain as the black frigid water drew her down. Her heavy clothing, soaked, was an iron weight about her body. In seconds the fiery tingling of her flesh changed to numbness. *No!*

Seconds seemed like forever. Jessy felt herself being pulled. Her head cleared water. She blinked icy lashes and saw Farley's stricken, yet determined face. He lay flat on the ice. His hard young fists caught in the ends of the muffler wound about her neck. He tugged, reached for her shoulder, her arm.

"*Jessy.*" Tears glinted at the corners of his eyes. "Jessy," he said again, "I'll get you out. Help me if you can. Don't be scared. Got to get you out—over here—thicker ice."

After a timeless agony of effort, Jessy, soaked and as cold as death, lay atop the ice. Using his elbows to propel him, Farley scooted backward, hands strong under her arms. He begged her to help him however she could. Words of encouragement and caring came in an unbroken flood. "I love you, Jessy Faber. Don't give up, Jessy. Oh, Jessy, we're gonna make it, you an' me. We'll make it, darling."

It seemed endless hours passed before they finally reached the snowy bank. Teeth chattering, Jessy tried to crawl up the incline on her own and couldn't. The icy water had frozen her strength away. Farley hugged her, half lifted her, onto the snow. He pushed. High on the bank at last, Jessy turned and saw Farley coming up behind her. Safe! Jessy sobbed with joy. Then, he slipped. Farley's arms flailed as he fell back onto the terrible ice. It splintered open beneath him. He sank from sight, down into the black water, came up again, went down.

"No," he chattered, coming up and seeing Jessy crawling back to help him, "I c-can g-get out."

She caught his hands, tried to pull, grew angry at her kitten-like weakness. A shroud of dark threatened to come over her. She fought, her blood like ice—she couldn't faint, she had to hold on! Farley's struggles grew weaker. His skin was so ghastly blue. *Hold on… hold on….*

HOW LONG FARLEY was in the frigid water and she in the snow, Jessy was later never sure. A tramp, she was told afterward, traveling toward Seena, had spotted them and hurried to help. She was unconscious. Farley was dead.

At the funeral she could not look at his parents. *Their only son.* Remorse closed her in, stilled any sympathetic words she might have offered them. The Baxters tried several times to see Jessy after that, but eventually gave up. And, Jessy's guilt about all of it grew deeper and deeper.

The hot little room in the back of the telephone office had become like an icebox while Jessy lay remembering. She sat up, overcome by a spasm of shivering, then warm tears flooded down her cheeks. "I wish I was home with my family," she whispered out loud. "Most of all I wish Farley and I hadn't gone out on the ice that day."

How could she go on in this place or anywhere?

Chapter 3

FOR A LONG TIME Jessy sat in the dark, her arms encircling her knees. Her tears dried. She didn't like feeling this way—sorry for herself. Others had worse problems, maybe. With a sigh, loud in the tiny room, she curled back under the sheet. Tomorrow might be a better day.

Mrs. Stuberg had promised to be in early, but it was nearly eleven-thirty when she came into the telephone office on feet that seemed unsure of where their next step should go. Her smile, greeting Jessy at the switchboard, was warm and friendly. "H'lo, Miss Faber, Jessamyn! How you doin', hon?"

After a slight hesitation, wondering at her boss' condition, Jessy told her, "Half the town is mad at me, that's how I'm doing. My first morning, too. I thought I had the switchboard all figured out last night, and I'm sure I do. But you wouldn't believe what's happened."

"A mess?" Gussie wagged her head, her expression gentle.

"Normal, normal, a girl's first time at the board. Tell me what you did to get folks' dander up. We'll see if there's permanent damage."

"This will sound silly," Jessy warned. Turning to look at the switchboard every few seconds, she explained, "A Mrs. McHugh tried to call a friend on another line to ask how long she should cook watermelon preserves. Her friend's line was busy, a long time. I couldn't interrupt. I tried to tell Mrs. McHugh how long Mama and I cook them, till they kind of jell, but she wouldn't listen. Her preserves scorched. She blamed me!"

"Well, of course," Gussie said mildly, "even if it ain't your fault. Next time, just butt in on the other conversation, don't be afraid. Tell 'em Mrs. McHugh's got trouble with her preservin'. That's all you got to do. Anything else happen?"

Seeing drops on the board, Jessy took time to put through two calls, hesitantly, and pulled the cords on three that were finished. Then she continued, "A rancher who said he lives down on the Cimarron River wanted to know the price of feed, *oats*, at the feedstore. The feedstore has no phone, and he said it was too far for him to come into town to find out. He thought I should be able to tell him, that it was my job to know. Is that true, will I be expected to know such things?"

"Y'betcha. And a whole lot more. Handlin' cords and ringin' keys ain't all of an operator's job. Folks expect Central to have answers to everything—big and little. When folks got an emergency, it'll be up to you to supply the miracle they want. That's how it is. An operator in a small town is as necessary to folks as a hub is to a wheel."

"Honestly?" That would be new for her, if it was true. Jessy gave her boss a searching look. The woman's serious expression set off a small warm glow inside Jessy, then she frowned and went on, "Another farmer called to ask me if I could see his hired man loafing out on the street. I could see him, across the street, from the farmer's description. But I didn't know if I should—"

"No *buts*. All part of a switchboard operator's work. You hang your head out the door and yell at the man, tell him to go on home, his boss needs him." Concern must still have shown on Jessy's face for Gussie asked worriedly, "You ain't quittin' on me?" She leaned forward. "There's lots to like about this job. You can do a peck of good for folks."

"No, I'm not quitting," Jessy replied. "I just want to know what's expected of me." She didn't want to go home. She wanted to learn this job, do it right. "If subscribers will put up with me, be patient, I'll keep trying."

"Good." Gussie sighed. "I hoped you'd feel that way. Lookit, you've had enough training for your first day. I want you to go around town this afternoon and meet folks. It'll make things easier for you if you know who's who and what's what."

Go out and introduce herself to strangers? Jessy felt a bit queasy. But if it was part of her job, she'd better do it. She sighed.

"I'll warn you," Gussie said, "folks gettin' to know *you*, that will be a different story. You're gonna be 'Central' to most everybody, they won't bother to know your name."

Jessy nodded that she understood. "What time would you like me to be back? I don't know what hours I'll be working yet—"

"You come back today when you're ready. From now on you'll get every other Sunday and every Tuesday, off. Noon and suppertimes I'll come spell you, and anytime one of us has something important to tend to, we can always trade. Twenty years ago I handled this board all by myself." She hiccupped. "But I ain't as young—or well—as I used ta' be."

"Today, are you sure—?" Jessy blushed.

After a thoughtful pause, Gussie said, "Lydia Pinkham's. I had to take a double spoonful of my tonic, Lydia Pinkham's, after breakfast. Made me a bit woozy for a while. I'm fine." She reached for the headset and gently shoved Jessy off the stool. "Go get your noon dinner."

✵

JESSY CROSSED THE STREET to Pierce's Pharmaceutical next door to the telephone office, after her meal at Mandy's. The druggist was arguing with an old woman who wanted medicine without a prescription. After a long wait, Jessy realized the disagreement was a ritual and not at all close to settlement. She'd have to introduce herself to the druggist some other day.

The proprietor of Burmann's Department Store was away in Kansas City on business. Struggling against being timid, Jessy managed to make herself known at the other stores. Simple words of welcome from the business people, and brief nods of acceptance, helped her feel more at ease.

She felt more like her normal self, going into the Hale Automobile Agency. Mrs. Stuberg had had many nice things to say about the owner, Lombard Hale. But she hesitated inside the large showroom.

"May I help you, Miss?" a smooth voice asked warmly. Then, a wide-shouldered, well-dressed older gentleman appeared from the back of the store, smiling at her.

"Mr.—Mr. Hale?" She smiled. "My name is Jessamyn Faber. I'm new in town, Mrs. Stuberg's new telephone operator. I'll be taking your calls and would—would like to be of any help that I can."

Well-groomed hands reached to clasp one of hers. "Nice to meet you, dear. I like to be of help, too. I am mayor of this town. For such a lovely girl—well, my dear—anything you need, anytime, call on me. We want you to be happy here in Ardensville." His gray eyes were strangely cool in spite of deep smile crinkles at the corners.

Jessy wasn't sure how she felt about him. She withdrew her hand as the mayor, in his rich, vibrant voice, set to asking her questions about her home and family.

"Good! Fine! Wonderful!" He exclaimed to her answers, making Jessy feel she was being given a test of sorts and was passing.

"I'm from farm stock myself," Lombard Hale told her. "On my daddy's side. I still ranch here and there to keep my hand in. But my heart is in this lovely little town." He waved crossed fingers. "Ardensville and I are like this. Fifty years ago, my mother's father—my grandfather, sold fine buggies and carriages from this very building."

Jessy smiled wider, hoping to look properly impressed.

Suddenly, over her shoulder, he saw something, and Jessy heard the door behind her open. Hale looked happy. "Anna Cora, dear, come here! Cecil, you, too. I want you to meet our new Central."

Jessy drew in a soft breath as she studied the pair coming to where she and Hale waited. They were—*different*. The fellow's legs were short for his long body. His heavy step caused an accumulation in his bulging pockets to jangle like bad music. A friendly smile came and went on his bony features as he faced Jessy.

"H'lo, Miss Central. I'm Cecil Kinglake." He turned and caught the hand of the girl who hovered behind his broad back. "Say how do you do to Central, Annie." Love and gentle encouragement filled his face as he pulled the girl forward.

"Hello, Central," Anna Cora whispered. A tiny, uncertain smile came to her face, then she looked down. Wispy light-brown hair fell forward, hiding her features. She looked thin in her loose, flowered dress.

The dress was designed for someone a lot older; maybe an older woman picked the girl's clothes for her, Jessy thought. "I'm happy to meet you, Anna. Cecil. I hope we see a lot of one another." She smiled.

Lombard Hale put an arm around Anna Cora's thin shoulder. He caressed the silky fabric of her sleeve, and he kissed her brow. Jessy stirred uncomfortably when his other arm went out to gather her in. "Miss Faber, dear, have you had your noon dinner?

Would you do my daughter and me the honor of going to lunch with the two of us?"

His daughter! "Th-that would have been nice, but I have eaten. Maybe Anna's friend would like my place?" Jessy smiled at Cecil. Her face turned hot when Hale shook his head slightly, saying nothing. Was Cecil being left out because he was Ardensville's handyman and gardener? Was the mayor that narrow-minded? Simple in the mind or not, Anna Cora and Cecil cared deeply for one another, anyone with eyes could see it.

"Sorry, thanks," Jessy said, more sharply this time. She couldn't see Anna Cora's face now, but from the wide grin on Cecil's face, being slighted was nothing new to him. "I have things to do. I'm glad I met all of you." She headed for the door, and the others came close behind her.

Outside on the sidewalk, Jessy turned for a last good-bye, and was mildly shocked when Mr. Hale dashed from behind her into the street, a furious frown on his face. The breeze ruffled the perfect set of his gray-brown hair. Jessy watched as he chased a single candy wrapper that bounced and flew along just out of his reach. He was attacking the bit of paper like—an enemy army almost, she thought.

Jessy moved on down the street, stopping now and then to look back over her shoulder. Lombard Hale held the retrieved scrap over his head in triumph.

That might explain a few things, Jessy decided. Ardensville was as neat as it was because of the mayor's love for the town. And because of Cecil Kinglake's hard labor doing the mayor's wishes, no doubt. Jessy shook her head. She might be imagining it, but the mayor seemed a touch odd.

Jessy took time out for a cold drink and a brief visit in Ardensville's second restaurant. She was strolling on and had stopped to gaze into a store window when a voice asked, "Shine, lady? Shine?"

A black man leaned against a large box seat intended for his shoeshine customers. Jessy looked down at her trim brown pumps, smiled and shook her head. "No. Thanks. Nice afternoon, isn't it?" There was no telephone connected with his shoebox business, but Jessy told him, "I'm Jessamyn Faber, the new telephone operator. Seeing the town."

He tipped his brown felt hat to her. "Name's Joe, Ma'am, Joseph Cooke. Hope you like our town."

"I do." Jessy walked on. She'd covered most of the business places and was now on a street of fine old two-story homes. She would wander now for fun, to see, to explore. She stood for a full minute before a flower-framed cottage, drinking it in. All the time she was little, she remembered, she had looked forward to growing up and having a husband and babies, living *happily ever after* in such a house. Then—Farley. Jessy felt suddenly, unbearably, tired.

She shaded her eyes and saw a small wooded lot not far ahead. She would rest a minute or two there and then go back.

It was cooler under the huge old sycamore trees. Jessy found a fallen log and sat down. With her mind deliberately empty and her eyes closed, she listened to the breezes singing softly overhead. Against her closed eyelids, caught unaware, she suddenly saw Farley's blue face, broken ice. In a single motion, she staggered to her feet and began to run.

She moved fast, blindly, tripping over stones and twigs in her path. The ruins of an old church hidden in the woods finally blocked her way and broke her flight. Jessy stared at it, as her inner hurt began to ease. The church roof was caved in, a shambles. Several walls of faded, crumbly brick still stood and they held cobwebby, yet beautiful, stained glass windows and a thick carved main door. Sun rays through the colored glass windows gave a glow over all.

Entranced, Jessy walked into the church, hardly noticing the debris, the scampering insects, underfoot. This was beautiful, but it didn't jibe with the rest of spotless Ardensville. Why hadn't

Lombard Hale ordered all this cleared away? Was the old church off-limits to the mayor, or did he let it be because the trees hid the ruins from sight?

She liked it. It felt kind of—healing. She ought to go back, though. Augusta might be wondering where she'd gone to, might need her. Another few minutes and she would go back.

A sound, like tiny fairy voices, made Jessy hesitate and listen. And soon two dark-haired little girls came toward her through the trees, talking. Their pitifully thin arms were loaded with limbs and twigs. Jessy's heart went out to them. "Hello!" she called out, "could you use some help?"

The gypsyish waifs froze. They crouched, looking about with fright until they spotted her standing next to the tree. "It's all right, I'll help you," Jessy consoled. To her astonishment, the smaller girl, about eight, dropped her load of wood and started to cry. The older girl, maybe ten, stared at Jessy in terror, then she stopped and quickly gathered up a few sticks of the dropped wood and added them to her own heavy load. She mouthed a blur of words to the younger child, and they fled back the way they had come.

Jessy watched them go in dumbfounded shock. Poor urchins. Why did they run from her? Her own little sisters, Laurel and Mitty, after the first few minutes of meeting a stranger, would be pawing the newcomer and chatting a blue streak.

Curiosity and concern pulled Jessy along the path the girls had taken.

Chapter 4

BEFORE LONG Jessy came to a shack that made her think of a shepherd's hut she'd seen in a picture in her European history book. The hut was wood, stones and clay and roofed with brush. The whole had a peasant look, from the house to the flat stones that made a kind of porch and walk in front. Jessy slipped behind a nearby sycamore tree and peeked out when childish voices came from inside the shack.

Blackened ground around the hut and the black interior wall she could see through the open door made her wonder if the shed had once held coal. A coal shed for the preacher's house and church, the parsonage long since gone? But home, now, to the little girls!

A goat, tied to a sapling near the door, picked at a clump of grass and eyed Jessy's hiding spot from time to time. Clothes hung from pegs inside the hovel. A corner of a rickety table showed. From where she stood, Jessy couldn't see a stove, but a nutlike aroma (cooking beans?) hung in the air.

The older girl, her shabby dress pinned together in front, came to the doorway of the hut. She looked back over her shoulder into the dark room and said in a singsong, playing-house kind of voice, "Baby, hear me? Lucian and Chris are working hard painting that man's chicken house. They will be hungry, Delphie, I mean *baby*. Let's get some dandelion greens, now, to have with Chris and Lucian's supper."

"All right, Althea—I mean *Mama*," a second play-acting voice answered. "I'm coming."

Puzzled, held there by a deepening curiosity, Jessy watched from behind the tree as they prepared to leave, the older girl with a basket on her arm. "Don't go so fast, Althea." The younger one trotted behind. "I—I mean—*Mama*."

Jessy decided to stay out of sight until they were gone. She didn't want to scare them again. On the way home, her mind was filled with thought about the little girls. Silently, she repeated over and over the names she'd heard: Althea, Delphie, Chris, Lucian. Of course the ten-year old was not the smaller girl's mother. But why were they working so hard at pretending?

She was reaching for the doorknob, back at the telephone office, when it came to her. *The dismal coal shed home was the responsibility of the two girls.* To red up, and they probably had to do the cooking and washing, too. For—who did they say? Lucian and Chris. It sounded like brothers. All that work. Unless they could pretend they were only playing house, and could stop anytime, it would be an awful burden for such little kids. That was it. She heaved a sigh. With the puzzle solved, she could put it out of her mind.

Except, she couldn't. After the first week, handling the switchboard was easy and the work actually tended toward monotony. Though there were occasional emergencies that made her feel helpful. Searching for something interesting to busy her mind, Jessy's thoughts often went back to the little girls in the woods hut. Why did they live there? Who were they, really? Why were they so afraid? She'd give a lot to know.

Maybe her boss, maybe Mrs. Stuberg, could tell her.

"Them orphans been living there about three months now," Gussie told Jessy. "Two boys and two girls. Dark-skinned, Greek, I think. Name's Salonika. Boys are older and ragged as sin. They do odd jobs, mostly for Lilli Miller at her boardin' house when Cecil can't."

"The girls were awfully bashful—no," Jessy corrected herself—"scared."

"Why not?" Gussie countered. "Them children are trespassin', I'd guess. Squattin' on somebody else's private property. They don't want to get caught."

"Maybe," Jessy sighed, "but I don't know—"

"Well, if you don't believe me," Gussie snorted, "talk to Lilli Miller. She oughta know about them if anybody does. They do for her."

"I'm sorry, it isn't that I don't believe you," Jessy said quickly. "It's just that—" she floundered for words. "I think I will talk to Miss Miller, sometime."

Gussie had told her not to worry about leaving the telephone office at night; everybody knew they were closed after eight or nine o'clock. It was more important, Gussie said, to be at the board early in the morning, when most folks were up and wanting to tend to business. The night she decided to see Lilli after work, Jessy passed Isaac Burmann locking up his department store.

"Central, halloo," he called to her.

"Hello, Mr. Burmann," Jessy answered, her tone forlorn. She bit her tongue, on the verge of asking the bearded storekeeper to please call her by name. Like Gussie'd said, she was called "Central" all the time. To have most folks thinking of her as a *tool* called Central made her feel empty, lonely. She'd rather be a *person*, Jessy Faber.

The major couldn't be faulted on this. When he placed a call, he not only called her by name, but most times he asked how she was, too, before he gave her the number he wanted.

The mayor's tidy habits about town were still cause for wonder, however. Through the plate glass window at work, she often saw him on the street picking up some scrap or other. Once she even saw him stop to dig out a dandelion that had poked up through a crack in the sidewalk. Jessy laughed softly, remembering.

At the Miller mansion, Jessy took the flight of steps, then caught her breath before she lifted the brass knocker. She let it drop twice. In a moment, the door was opened by a young woman in a blue butterfly-print dress. Light from a hall chandelier above turned Lilli Miller's coronet of white-blonde braids into a kind of halo. She tipped her head to one side and smiled at Jessy as though trying to decide if she knew her.

"May—may I help you?"

Jessy plunged. "I know this is a silly hour to come calling, but I feel I know you, sort of, from your calls, Miss Miller. I've been wanting to ask you about something—" She hesitated and drew a breath. "If you don't want a visitor this late—?" Jessy started to turn.

"Wait a minute for goodness sake!" Lilli laughed. She grabbed Jessy's arm. "Please come in. And call me Lilli. You're Central, aren't you?"

"Yes." Jessy sighed. "I'm *Central*." She followed the girl into a small parlor off the entry hall. "My name, though, is Jessamyn Faber—Jessy." For the next few seconds the room captured her attention. Lilli's mahogany parlor furniture looked beautiful with the deep-rose drapes and upholstery and the oriental rug.

"I do believe you like my old house," Lilli commented in her throaty voice. "Look all you want, Central—*Jessamyn*—but please don't notice how old and worn everything is."

"Oh, don't apologize for such a lovely house," Jessy told her. She took the settee Lilli motioned her to. "I've wanted to meet you," she told Lilli then. "I heard you own this boarding house and run it yourself." She pushed the other things Augusta had said to the back of her mind and went on quickly, "You're the youngest businesswoman I've ever met."

Sitting across from Jessy, Lilli shrugged. "I'm twenty. About three years older than you, right? I don't intend to do this forever," she explained. "My Aunt Martha left me this gorgeous place; if I had good sense I suppose I would put it up for sale and go back to St. Louis. But it doesn't seem fair to Aunt Martha, somehow. I loved her, and we both loved this house. So I rent rooms to boarders to pay the upkeep."

"What else would you like to do?" Just looking at Lilli, Jessy had the feeling that the answer would be interesting.

Lilli looked toward the ceiling, her hazel eyes shone. "Oh, well, if I could earn enough money from renting these rooms, I'd like to go back to St. Louis to college, maybe. Study journalism. World history." She made a small motion of her hand to dismiss the subject. "Can I get you something Cen—Jessamyn? Lemonade? Iced tea?" Her cheeks dimpled with deviltry. "A little cooking sherry?" she asked in a low voice, "some wine?"

Jessy couldn't help laughing. "Thank you, nothing. And I have to confess, I'm a plain country girl; I don't drink spirits."

"I don't either," Lilli said with a grin, "so that gives us something in common. I don't smoke, don't swear, I can't even get very interested in chewing gum!" She giggled. "But please keep all this a secret from your boss."

"What?" Jessy was mystified. "Why?"

"Because the most fun I have in this dull little town is pretending to Gussie Stuberg that I am a scandalous St. Louis flapper. She'd be horribly disappointed in the real Lilli Miller. One day in the drugstore she caught me buying a copy of *True Story*, that new love confession magazine. She's believed the worst about me ever since. It's fun for both of us—gives dash to our days."

"Oh, Lilli."

They laughed companionably, then Lilli said, "Kid, tell me about you, now. What's it like, being a telephone operator? Is it hard?"

"It's not hard." Jessy shook her head. "The switchboard itself is really easy. It's the people I handle calls for that make problems. I get blamed for poor connections. If somebody asks when the train is due, I get blamed if the train is late. Like that. The rest of the time it's kind of slow and quiet."

"People listen in on one another's calls, don't they?"

Jessy laughed and nodded. "That's when I have to tell the eavesdroppers, with their receivers down all along the line, that they're weakening circuits and please hang up. You can hear a soft *click-click-click* as they hang up their phones. Some subscribers argue though. They think they should get to listen in. Party line eavesdropping is entertainment for quite a few people."

"What a job!" Lilli said huskily. In another minute she asked, "Jessy, didn't you say you wanted to ask me something?"

Jessy grew sober. "It's about the orphan family living in the church woods. I was told the boys do odd jobs for you? Could you tell me something about them? I tried to be friendly but only managed to scare the little girls."

Lilli shook her head. "The Salonika kids don't talk much, except to each other, Jessy. From things I've heard the boys say, I think they've come from Colorado. Lucian must be about fifteen; his brother, Christopher is twelve. You've seen the sisters, Althea and Delphine." Lilli shrugged. "That's really all I know about them. Although"—she was silent a moment—"I've had a feeling they are running from something. Or, they are being—I don't know—*bothered.*

Jessy leaned forward with her chin in her palm, her elbow on her knee. "I wonder about their folks, and I wonder why they live in that shack in the woods? I understand that they might not have the right to be there. Maybe somebody is being mean to them, trying to scare them off."

Again, Lilli shrugged. "Who knows? I tried to get Lucian to move them all into my carriage house, empty out back. But he's proud. Won't accept anything he thinks looks like charity. Maybe you'll have better luck trying to help them, Jessy."

"Thanks. I can't seem to get them out of my mind. I guess the girls make me think of my own little sisters." For the next half-hour Jessy told Lilli about the Fabers—Mama and Papa and their beloved Ranch. About her older sister Willow, who'd recently wed Reid Evans. About her younger brothers—sturdy, hard-working Walsh; and carefree, venturesome Adan, and about reckless little Clay. And her younger sisters Laurel and Mitt. Jessy's voice grew thick with feeling, talking about home.

"I'd give my soul for such a family," Lilli said. "I was an only child. My parents died when I was little, and I was reared by my grandmother. She's gone now, too. Don't you miss your family?"

Jessy had trouble answering. "A—a lot more than I thought I would. I get a letter from home every week, but it isn't like being there.

"Well, then, why do you live here in Ardensville?"

Jessy blinked away the sting in her eyes and looked aside. "It—it's a long story." She looked at Lilli. "And it is getting late. But I've liked talking to you tonight, very much. We—we can talk more, another time, all right?" Jessy waited, hoping Lilli would understand.

"We have all the time in the world," Lilli said quietly. Seconds later, she said with an impish smile, "In the meantime, let's do some fun things, the two of us, when we're both free? Take in a movie. We might even scare up a couple of fellows, though prospects aren't too impressive in Ardensville.

There could be a hundred nice fellows available in Ardensville and it wouldn't make a difference to her, Jessy thought, because of Farley. But she didn't say so because she didn't want to sound like a wet blanket. Instead she smiled and stood up. "We'll see. I'm glad we're going to be friends, Lilli. Thanks for making me welcome."

"You're staying in that little box in back of the telephone office, aren't you?" Lilli commented, leading the way to her front door. "How come you don't take one of my rooms? I have a third-floor room, small, but it's pretty and the rent won't bankrupt you—"

Jessy smiled. "The room at the telephone office is still cheaper, it comes with the job." She hesitated on the steps outside. "I like it there, Lilli. And I'm handy in case of an emergency. Although I've been here almost a month and there hasn't been one at night, yet."

"Listen, kid, if you're expecting something really razzle-dazzle to happen in this one-horse town, don't." Lilli sniffed. "Most of the time Ardensville is as solemn as a graveyard. I could die here. I really ought to go back to St. Louis." She sighed and waved a small hand, her bracelets jangling. "Not yet, though. 'Night, Jessy. Glad you came by. Do it again, soon."

"Good-night, Lilli. I'll see you."

The air had cooled, and Jessy hugged herself as she hurried along the dark street. She hadn't found out as much as she'd hoped to about the Salonika orphans. But she now had a friend near her own age in Ardensville.

And soon, on her day off, she'd try again to get the little Salonika girls to talk to her.

Chapter 5

ALTHOUGH SHE TRIED to make others, Gussie and Lilli mostly, believe she was completely happy in the back room at the telephone office, Jessy couldn't fool herself. At night, especially, the room was like a lonely cell. Nightmares still came, too easily. She would wake with her teeth clenched and her body bathed in perspiration.

It helped sometimes to take a short walk, even very late. On one such night a kitten hurtled itself at Jessy from where it had been sitting by a lamppost. It curled about her ankles, mewing piteously. "Just a minute!" Jessy laughed softly, trying to step aside. She hesitated, then stopped and caught the kitten in her hands. It was hardly more than bones, covered with long fuzzy hair.

"Poor thing," she cooed, heading back to the telephone office with the kitten in her arms. "I don't think I have a thing to feed you—well, maybe some crackers and cheese." Back home on the farm there were always animals to name and love. Lots of pets. "I want you," Jessy whispered, hugging the kitten up close to her neck, her chin rubbing its fur. "We can be company for one another. Outcasts, together."

A short distance from the telephone office and her room, Jessy saw a small shadowy figure dash from the opposite side of the street to pound on the telephone office door.

"Wake up! Please!" a hoarse, boy's voice shouted. "Central, you got to get up, quick—!"

Jessy gasped and broke into a run, holding the kitten close. A moment later she was beside the boy, nearly breathless. "I'm here," she panted, "what's wrong?"

"Fire!" he cried, looking up at her. He rattled the doorknob, "Miss Central, you got to get in there and call out the volunteers, the fire department."

"All—all right." Jessy was already fumbling her key into the lock. "Where is the fire?"

"Church woods, ma'am, fire's in the church woods."

Jessy went stone cold at his words. She sagged against the door, and it opened. "Wait! Don't leave yet," Jessy implored when she saw the boy turn to go. "Here, hold my cat." She dashed inside, yanked the light cord, raced to the board and snatched up her headset. Against her mind's eye, she pictured the memorized telephone numbers for the few men who were Ardensville's fire department. Jessy rang them one after the other to give her curt message, "Fire. Corner of Tenth and Liberty. In the church woods."

When her part was done, Jessy's chin quivered and she felt sick. *The little girls.* The firemen had to get there in time, get the fire out. She turned to the waiting boy who'd come inside to stand behind her. She saw now in the light that he was black. "I can't leave the board," she told him. "I never should have gone out tonight, but I have to know if the little children who live in those woods are all right. Did you see the fire? Just where in the woods was it?"

"Didn't see it myself, ma'am," the boy said solemnly, stroking the gray kitten. "Old Mrs. McCarthy yelled to us out her side window, said she could see this little red glow over in the church woods. Mrs. McCarthy is crippled, she lives next door to me and my papa and brother. I came here fast as I could. Papa and Edwin went on to the fire to help put it out."

"Good." Jessy felt so happy she could cry. Someone was there. She asked with a tremulous sigh, "What's your name?"

"Harry Cooke, ma'am." He shuffled from one foot to the other. "Is that all? I'd better go on now and find Pop and Edwin, see if they got the fire out." He set the kitten down on the floor.

"Your father must be the bootbl—Is Joe Cooke your dad?" The boy nodded. "I met him not long after I came to Ardensville," Jessy told the boy. "Harry," she drew a long breath, "I'd consider it a special favor—could you or your father find out about the children who live in that shack in the church woods, if they are all right? Could you? And would you come back tonight and tell me?"

"Sure. That ain't no trouble." He hesitated a second to see if she had anything else to tell him, then he was gone.

Still shaky, Jessy absentmindedly picked up the kitten. It meowed. "I promised you something to eat, didn't I?" She held the kitten up for a better look and a memory flickered briefly across her thoughts. "With those dark blue eyes, and these boots," she stroked the tiny white feet with a finger, "There's only one name for you *Cowboy*. All right?"

She brought a small braided rug from her room and placed it near the switchboard, crumbled some cheese for the kitten and the little animal attacked it, growling. "Now shush," she soothed, "nobody's going to take your dinner, Cowboy. Tomorrow you can have milk."

A short time later, Joseph Cooke knocked on the telephone office door. "The fire is out, Miss," he told Jessy. "Nobody hurt. My boy, Harry, said you want to know about it."

Jessy felt instant relief. "The fire didn't get out of hand, then? Does anybody know how it started?"

He seemed careful with his answer. "The fire didn't amount to much. A little shack in the woods caught fire, but there wasn't hardly any damage before I got there and put the fire out. Nobody hurt serious, though a little girl got a burn on her arm."

Still he hadn't said how the fire started. "It was an accident, wasn't it?" she asked, "not set on purpose—to hurt the children there—?"

"The volunteer firemen thought it was a prank," Joe said dryly. "Some smart aleck being careless with a cigarette."

"What did the Salonika children say?"

"Nothing, not a word all the time I was there. They was scared, though, so scared they just froze up after I helped them put the fire out. The firemen were a little rough on them at first, wondering if they'd been playing with matches. Maybe the firemen were out of sorts because there wasn't something for them to do—I had the fire out before they got there."

"Good heavens, I hope they don't blame me," Jessy cried. "And anyway that fire could have gotten out of hand, someone could have been hurt worse. I keep thinking I might not have been here—"

Joe shook his head, "You did your job. And everything's okay." He put on his hat. "I have to get home to my boys."

"Thank you for coming by," Jessy murmured. If the fire was small, why didn't she feel better, satisfied? Was she fidgety and worried for no reason? Since most of her days here were quiet, maybe she made too much of a thing when it did happen.

In spite of her resolve to leave well enough alone, when Gussie Stuberg relieved her at twelve noon next day, Jessy made her way to the church woods. She'd feel better if she could see for herself that the children were all right.

When the coal shed came in sight, Jessy hesitated behind the sycamore tree. She stared, biting her lip to keep from crying out.

One lower wall of the shack was a charred mess. The gypsylike girls and a boy about twelve were in the yard. With a hopelessly blackened rag, Althea wiped at the soot on a small table, then she moved to clean rickety chairs. The boy hung a sodden blanket across a short rope tied between trees.

The littlest girl, Delphine, suddenly dropped the bundle of rags she carried and sat down in the mud in front of the hovel. With her head back, she sobbed around the thumb in her mouth, "Mama, Mama, please come. Please!"

"Hush, baby," the ten-year-old turned to say to her sister, "I'm your mama now. I say to hush your crying this minute. Lucian will be home today. He can't see this. You know we have to clean our house before he gets home. Hear me, Delphine? You take the wet clothes and hang 'em around on the bushes so they'll dry out."

"I hadn't ought to've thrown so much water around, I guess, me and that black man," Jessy heard the boy say. "But it don't matter, and we'll get the house fixed again. There are some big sheets of tin I can get at the town dump. I saw some bricks and boxes and things like that there, too. We will just fix this place right back up again. 'Can't scare us away!' That's what Lucian'll say."

The younger girl stopped crying. "Why can't we go home, Chris, back where we used to live? I want to go home. Mama and Daddy is maybe there."

"Delphie, you know better," Chris answered with a deep sigh. "Our home isn't there anymore, you know that. Nothing's there. Mama and Daddy are dead. You remember."

Listening behind the tree, Jessy felt an ache filling her throat.

"Lucian likes it here, he says Ardensville is a good town for us to stay in," Althea explained to her little sister. She wiped the chairs with vigor, her small shoulders thrown back. "We can't keep on walking all our lives. If we don't budge, Lucian says, folks will give up trying to scare us off. We can stay."

The boy, Chris, spoke, "We're staying here, regardless."

"I want my mother, regar'less," the little girl on the ground insisted with a dry sob. But she stood up, picked up the spilled rags and moved toward the bush where Jessy remained hidden, giving Jessy an idea. Delphie began to spread a wet shirt over the limbs of the bush, and Jessy held her breath.

When the child came close enough to touch, Jessy used her softest tone, "Peek-a-boo, honey. Let me help you." She caught a small arm and held on. The others wouldn't run if she held their little sister. Jessy stepped into full view with the squirming Delphie. "It's all right," she touched Delphie's hair with her free hand, "I'm not going to hurt you."

Chris and Althea's eyes went wild with fear, but they didn't move as Jessy gave them a searching, earnest look. "I'm the telephone operator in Ardensville," she told them, "who handled the call about the fire you had here last night. My name is Jessy Faber. I'd like to help you."

The children were silent, motionless. A sudden small pain in Jessy's thigh surprised her. She looked down and saw Delphie trying to bite her leg a second time. "No, please!" Jessy cried, attempting to laugh. "Don't hurt me. I wouldn't hurt you."

"You are," Delphine sobbed, "you're hurting my arm."

Jessy looked closer at the arm she held. The red skin was beginning to blister. "Oh, no! It's your burned arm. Honey, I'm really sorry." With no thought except to comfort the child, Jessy knelt and drew the stiffened little girl against her. "There, there," she said, and patted Delphie's back.

Slowly, the stiffness left the small body, the girl leaned against Jessy. She felt a warm thrill and after a moment, she picked Delphie up and started toward Chris and Althea, who could have been playing a game of statues.

"I came here to help you," she said again. "That's all."

"Why?" Chris demanded to know.

"Because," Jessamyn halted in front of him. "I have brothers and sisters at home like you. I—I miss them."

A kind of spring seemed to let go in the girl, Althea. In the measuring look she gave Jessy there was doubt, but acceptance, too. "We need soap," she said.

"I'll get soap," Jessy agreed.

"We need salve to put on Delphie's arm so it don't get 'fected. She's the only one of us got hurt. She was asleep by the wall that burned."

"I'll get salve."

Chris finally took a step, toward her. "We can pay you," he said, "we ain't beggars. Our brother Lucian has been away working on a hay ranch for four days. We'll be practically rich when he gets home."

"Of course," Jessy said, sitting down on one of the chairs Althea had been cleaning, Delphine in her lap. "I understand. I'll bring the things back here tonight, late, when the telephone office is closed." She hated to be away, in case of an emergency, but the only nighttime emergency she'd had had happened right here. They needed her. And it wouldn't take long.

Christ grunted, "We have to know for sure it's you when you come back. Make a call like a mourning dove, when you come. Sometimes people come in the night and throw rocks at our house while we're asleep. They wake us with scary yelling. The fire last night wasn't an accident. Somebody set it on purpose; I'll show you." He went into the hovel and came out carrying a stick that was charred on the end. "I found this. Smell it." He held it out to Jessy. "Smells like coal oil."

Jessy shivered, unable to believe what he was saying, yet scared, too. "W-why would anyone do such a th-thing?"

Chris shrugged. "I don't know. But I think Lucian does. He won't tell us; he says it will stop, not to worry."

"Has your big brother gone to the police?" Jessy asked. "They have to know about this fire. Did he tell them about the rock throwing?"

"Ardensville hasn't got a policeman, or a sheriff," Chris told her. "Lucian checked one time."

"Good grief, I think you're right." She hadn't thought about it before. "I haven't heard anything about a police department; no calls for the police. That is odd."

Chris explained, "Ardensville ain't never had a real bad crime, a man told Lucian. So they don't need police here. The man said there's always the county sheriff over at Macloud could be called. He's generally too busy to come for little things, but for a robbery or murder, he'd come. The little stuff the mayor takes care of."

"The mayor?" Jessy repeated thoughtfully. "Has your brother talked to Lombard Hale about all this? Mr. Hale is real nice, even if he acts a bit strange. It seems like he would put a stop to this. If Mr. Hale knew, people wouldn't bother you."

"Will you tell the mayor for us?" Althea asked as she joined them.

Chris looked at his sister with pleased surprise. He turned to Jessy, "Would you, Central?"

"Me?" She couldn't, no.

"You're somebody important, *Central*." Chris answered quickly. "Everybody knows Central. The mayor would listen to you."

Jessy felt herself blushing. Her conscience was too big for her own good. Getting her into hot water she didn't need. "All right," she was shocked to hear herself say. "I—I, if you want me to, I'll talk to the mayor. I'll just…I don't know. But we'll get this stopped, somehow."

Her mind leaped ahead, dizzily. What was she promising? She hugged Delphine and stood her on her feet. "My lunch hour must be almost over. I have to go. But I'll be back tonight with the soap and salve." The three of them grinned, making her glad at least for the moment that she'd given them her word. Delphine acted as though she didn't want her to leave.

As it was, Jessy was a few minutes late getting back to the telephone office. She kept Mrs. Stuberg for a moment, asking her about Ardensville's lack of police protection. Gussie readjusted her flowered hat down close over her face, and repeated almost word for word what Chris had told Jessy. "Don't need none. Ain't never been a murder or serious robbery in Ardensville. We got Mayor Hale and his town council to take care of our few hassles." Mumbling something about a dry throat, Gussie waved good-bye to Jessy and ambled out of the telephone office.

A busy fifteen minutes passed at the board, then Jessy made her own call to the Hale automobile agency. When she was told Mr. Hale was not in, she felt a wash of relief. She wasn't sure what she wanted to say to him, though it should be easy, and she'd promised the children. Jessy next rang the Hale mansion, picturing as she waited for someone to answer, the massive colonial house at the end of Main Street—where Gussie said the mayor and his daughter, Anna Cora, lived.

No one answered after several rings. Sorry this time, Jessy reluctantly reached to withdraw the cords and in that same second she heard the receiver being lifted at the other end.

"H-hello?" a timid voice asked, "hello, is—is anybody there?"

"Anna Cora? It's me, Jessy Faber. I—I'd like to talk to your father. Is he in?"

There was a moment of silence, then the small voice queried, "Central?"

"Yes, Anna. This is—Central. Jessamyn Faber. I'd like to talk to Mr. Hale, please?" Jessy waited, wondering if the silence that followed meant that Anna Cora had left the line.

Suddenly, Anna Cora's voice came again, softly, "Father went to the hotel to talk to a man. He took Cecil. It's a meeting, I think they said."

"All right, Anna, that's fine," Jessy told her. "Will you tell your father I called? I'll try again, because I'd really like to talk to him."

There was a murmur of an answer Jessy couldn't make out and a click as Anna Cora hung up the telephone.

It was a full afternoon at the switchboard. Among the usual calls were two public announcements. Jessy rang six longs then told all those picking up their phones that there would be a Methodist church supper—each family was to bring their own table service, a hot dish, and dessert. The second announcement was about a sale on beef roasts at Wolverton's Grocery. Jessy was careful to give the correct price, fifteen cents a pound.

At Jessy's suppertime, Gussie Stuberg reported for work giggling like a schoolgirl. "Are you all right, Mrs. Stuberg?" she asked. "You seem a bit—dizzy, again."

"I couldn't be better, sweetie!" Gussie chortled. "Had a case of nerves earlier today. But I took my medicine, and I'm fit as a fiddle now, thanks to *Lydia!*"

Jessy shook her head. If Lydia Pinkham's tonic was what Mrs. Stuberg had been drinking, the woman had dosed herself with more than enough. She sighed. Should she stay and send her tipsy boss back home? No, she really ought to buy the salve for Delphine's arm. The burn could get infected if it wasn't treated. "I'll get a bowl of soup, run a quick errand, and be back," she told Mrs. Stuberg. "You can manage?"

THE INSTANT SHE stepped into the telephone office, later, Jessy knew she shouldn't have left it. Enveloped in a fit of laughter, Gussie Stuberg rolled on the switchboard stool like a humpty-dumpty egg about to slip off. An empty brown bottle lay on the floor by the stool. With a wild gesture, Gussie opened a key, "Are you through, are you through?" she shouted. "You ain't? Too bad!" She yanked the connection and swung the cord around her head like a lariat.

"Mrs. Stuberg, please, stop this—" Jessy ran forward, frightening Cowboy off his little rug.

Gussie took another call. "You want to talk to Kelly Smith? Nah you don't." She shook her head, "You want to talk to Mr. Lombard Hale, nice man. Now, you talk to him." Gussie made the connection. She rocked dangerously on the stool and roared with laughter.

"Mrs. Stuberg!" Jessy rushed to catch the woman before she fell. "What are you doing?"

"Hav-havin-'" Gussie belched, loud; she looked up at Jessy with a confidential smile. "Havin' the time of my life, honey. I got folks talkin' to other folks they ain't spoke to in years. Helpin' people to be friendly, get to know one another. An' I stopped some a' them old gossips been tyin' up the lines for years. I'm teaching 'em—"

"But you can't," Jessy protested. She struggled to hold the woman upright on the stool. Cowboy came back to brush against her ankles. "You can't do this. Mrs. Stuberg, how much have you had to drink? We'd better get you to Mandy's for some coffee and supper. Come now, please, give me the headset."

Chapter 6

GUSSIE STUBERG rolled her eyes, childlike. "I had fun today," she confessed. "Can't understand it. Usually this job ain't but a ol' bother. Must be my Lydia Pinkham's makes me feel so good."

"It isn't just a tonic that's got you like this," Jessy said firmly, "and coffee is what you need. I've got to get this switchboard straightened out." She helped her boss toward the door. "Be careful, don't step on my kitty." Jessy looked nervously for traffic. "Mrs. Stuberg, get yourself across the street to Mandy's, please."

Gussie waved. "Bye-bye." Jessamyn watched the woman meander across the street and through the cafe door before she heaved a sigh and hurried back to the switchboard. Well, she'd taken this job with her eyes wide open—but it wouldn't be easy undoing the mess Gussie's "good time" had surely wrought. Jessy swallowed back her giggles and went to work.

"Of course, I'll ring Kelly Smith, right away. Yes, this is Jessy, the other operator. Mrs. Stuberg is very sorry, she—she isn't herself today. Yes, I know what happened—"

It took Jessy nearly half an hour to correct connections and soothe tempers. She apologized over and over for her boss' behavior. To one party she explained, "No, I can't fire her. Mrs. Stuberg owns the telephone company. I work for her."

WHO WOULD BELIEVE such a thing could happen, Jessy wondered, making her way to the church woods with the salve and other things after the switchboard was quiet that night. Still, she was glad she had plenty to do. She didn't want time—time for remembering, hurting because she couldn't undo things. With her mind preoccupied, Jessy forgot to use caution, and as she neared the coal shed, a short burly figure shot out of it to bar her way.

"Stop!" a young man's voice ordered.

It must be Lucian, the oldest, home from the hayfields. "Lucian," she said in a hollow voice, "I'm not one of those—others. My name is Jessamyn Faber. I'm the Ardensville telephone operator. Chris and Althea know me. They must have told you I was coming. I have medicine for Delphie's burned arm."

"We don't need you. Get on away from here," the husky voice ordered. The boy spoke good English, with only a trace of accent.

After a moment, Jessy tried again, "Lucian, I understand. I know you've had trouble—problems with others coming here. *I'm* here because I care about your brother and sisters—and you. Can't I come in now, please?" She moved through the shadows toward him.

"I have a rock in my hand," Lucian's sullen voice warned. "I'll heave it if you take another step."

A rock! Jessy stopped, ready to run. In that second a voice from inside the shed intervened. It was Althea, first timid, then demanding, "We know that girl out there, Lucian, that's Jessy.

She came by here at noon. We know she's all right. She's nice. We have to trust her, if she brought medicine for Delphine's arm. Let the girl come in here, Lucian!"

"Yes," Chris' voice agreed from inside the shed, "let her in, Lucian. Delphie wants her, she's crying for her, Luc."

Jessy swallowed. "Lucian, please?"

A long time seemed to pass. "Come in, then, this time." The rough voice sounded terribly lonely and worried, Jessy thought, for a boy his age. "But we don't need you to bother us again."

Trembling, Jessy went to lift the scrap of blanket that served now as a door to the coal shed. Althea and Chris threw her glad, nervous grins. Delphine rushed and threw her arms about Jessy's waist. Jessy sighed and looked over her shoulder at their fifteen-year-old brother who had followed her in.

Lucian Salonika wasn't as tall as she. Like the younger children, his skin was a mahogany tan below thick, beautiful black hair. In spite of the frostiness in his brown eyes and the grim set of his mouth, he was handsome. He nodded at the package Jessy held while she hugged Delphie. "Leave the medicine if you want to, but you go."

"No!" This time it was Delphine who protested. Fiery as a banty chicken she faced her older brother. "Jessy is my friend. Let her be, Lucian, Jessy is going to fix my sore arm." Delphine stepped back and poked her arm up at Jessy.

Jessy smiled in nervous apology. "I—I think you are overruled, Lucian." She watched him, feeling sorry for him, yet admiring him at the same time. He stalked to a chair and sat down, his brown eyes still plainly distrusting her.

"Althea," Jessy pretended now to ignore Lucian, "is there warm water in your teakettle? Good. Bring me some in a pan? I brought antiseptic soap. And some cheesecloth to wash Delphie's arm with; we'll use any leftover for bandage." She planted a kiss on the little girl's forehead. "I'll try not to hurt you." She smiled at the younger boy, Chris. "There are some apples and raisin cookies in the sack, too. Will you get them out for us?"

JESSY MADE several half-hearted attempts, in the next few days, to reach Lombard Hale to talk to him about the Salonikas. Yet, each time she called, the mayor was too busy to talk to her. If he wasn't so gracious about it, Jessy decided, she might think he was avoiding her on purpose.

On her days off, Jessy went to the movies with Lilli, or they stayed home and had long sisterly talks. She couldn't talk yet about Farley, but spending time with Lilli was a help for her homesickness.

She also visited the Salonika children on a regular basis, sharing their bread, cheese pies, and coffee. They too had long talks. After the night she first treated Delphine's arm, there was no mention from Lucian that she couldn't come again. But it was days, Delphine's arm was practically healed, before Lucian himself opened up and talked to her with trust.

It was a late-summer afternoon. Jessy sat with the Salonikas on a fallen log in a sun-splashed clearing in their woods. She had brought Cowboy along for her Sunday off outing, and the gray kitten's antics delighted the children.

Lucian was telling about their parents. "They never went to school one day in their lives. They were told that in America they wouldn't need schooling. There'd be machine tending they could do for high pay. That's why they left Greece to come to America."

What courage his parents must have had, to leave everything familiar to come to a strange, new country. Like her own parents. Papa was born in Sweden, Mama in France. Delphine moved closer against Jessy's side, on the log. "Mama and Papa died in Colorado," the little girl said quietly.

Jessy squeezed Delphine; she let a hand rest on Althea's knee next to hers. "What happened?" she asked Lucian.

He sighed. "Mama, and Papa, and me—I lied about my age—we worked in a steel mill at Pueblo, Colorado. We lived in a tent by the Arkansas River. Two years ago, it began to rain hard around the first of June. It rained like that for days. Everybody was ordered to move to high ground, the Arkansas River was getting higher and higher."

Lucian looked into the sycamore's deep leaves, his adam's apple bobbing in his throat as he went on, "We were getting our things together to leave on the third night of rain. The—the flood broke through a—a breakwater west of the city." The brown eyes looked tortured. "A-a wall of water crashed through town, the streets." The boy looked at his feet and shook his head. "Horses, cars, masses of trash, *people*, everything was caught in it."

Jessy hated seeing the pain in his face. "If you don't want to talk about it, Lucian…." She watched Chris walk away to sit with Cowboy in his lap at the base of a nearby tree.

"There isn't much more to tell. The lights went out," Lucian said. "People were crazy in the dark, driving like madmen, leaning on their horns, hitting people running away on foot, or on horseback. Mama and Papa sent us away to higher ground with some other millworkers. Our parents—stayed and helped. A hundred people drowned that night in the flood of the Arkansas. Mama and Papa—too" He shuddered visibly. "When it was over, twelve foot of water was over the whole town. Now they have flood control, it can't happen again."

Poor young'uns. Jessy's whole being ached for them. "I'm so sorry," she whispered. "It must have been awful. How—how did you get here—to Ardensville?"

"We walked," Chris answered, coming to stand in front of Jessy. "Sometimes we would stop and live in a town for quite a spell. Lucian and me, we would do odd jobs for money, or for fruit and vegetables, some bread. We been walking most of the time since I was ten, for two years."

"And you don't want to move anymore," Jessy said. "I don't blame you."

Lucian motioned in the direction of town. "Mama and Papa would like this clean, pretty town for the girls to grow up in. We're all going to go to school. Our parents wanted us to get schooling more than anything else in the world. Odd jobs here don't pay as much as the mill did, but it gives us time to go to school. We'll get by, till all of us are educated."

What if the Salonikas did live in an abandoned coal shed on an old vacant lot? Were they hurting anyone, really? Lucian might not want to tell her, but Jessy asked, cautiously, "Do you know who's pestering you? Who's trying to drive you out?" She hesitated, thoughtful. "And is there a chance the things that've happened here were—only accidents?"

For a minute Lucian eyed Jessy, his look impatient, then angry. "Miss Faber, don't you know a *band of crummy little foreigners* when you see them?" With a violent motion he reached into his pocket and yanked out a crumpled paper. "This is the latest message we got, and it didn't come by mail! It was fastened to a rock as big as my fist."

Jessy's own hands began to shake when she read what was scrawled in ink on the paper: *You crummy little foreigners weren't wanted wherever you came from. You aren't wanted in Ardensville, either. Get out!*

"This must be a joke," Jessy said. "No decent person would write such a thing. Tear it up. Forget about it."

"Joking?" Lucian's laugh crackled harshly. "Peppering our house with rocks in the middle of the night? Throwing a torch on our house?"

Jessy shivered. He was right. "What are you going to do? All of you could be hurt. This can't go on!"

"I'll tell you this much," Lucian said staunchly, his fist doubled, "we won't run. Nobody has a right to chase us off. I have proof it's all right for us to be here."

"Proof?"

He nodded. "This lot, these woods, is owned by a lady who lives in Denver. Our Papa saved her son's life, at the time of the flood. He was Papa's boss." Lucian brought out a second paper, which he unfolded carefully. "This is Mrs. Pickering's written permission for us to live here. Her son, Jim Pickering, told me about Ardensville and he got his mother's permission for us."

Chris spoke, "Jim Pickering gave us train money to come here, but we were robbed."

Althea told Jessy, "Mr Pickering thought there was a parsonage here, where a preacher used to live. But somebody had torn it down. We didn't care," her small chin lifted. "We moved into the coal shed, and we're fixing it up nice."

"Those people who helped, the Pickerings," Jessy said slowly, "it seems odd that they sent you here. I'd have thought they would look after you where you were, in Pueblo."

"Oh, they wanted us to stay in Colorado," Lucian told her. "We did for a while. Mama and Papa—it happened—there. We couldn't put it out of our minds, so close. The little girls were having bad dreams every night—we didn't want to stay there."

"So you came here." Running away from tragic death, just as she had. Jessy finished reading the letter of permission through a blur. Her head hurt. She handed the note back to Lucian for safekeeping. "Thank you for telling me all this. I want to help, Lucian." After all, they were helping her, keeping her from feeling so alone, remembering…. "Your letter will solve the trouble, I'm sure. You have a right to be here, and we have to let people know. Whoever is bothering you is dead wrong. They may get into serious trouble over this."

"Do you think you can find out who it is? Maybe you've heard something at the switchboard, or around town? And didn't think about it, before? If you know who it might be, I'll just show him, or them, the letter. Whenever they *visit*, the cowards don't show theirselves, or give me a chance to talk to them."

"I'm sorry, Lucian, if I have heard anything, I haven't paid attention. I just can't imagine anyone wanting to be so mean to you—from the start it hasn't made sense to me."

How could she find out who was doing it? Where ought she to start? Again, Jessy thought of the mayor, Lombard Hale. This time, the skin on the back of her neck crawled, a sudden chill zigzagged through her. What if *he* was the one? It would be like the mayor to think these kids were clutter, trash, and want them out of *his town!* Hale himself might have written that note. Alone, or maybe there were others in this....

She was doing it again, brewing a storm in a teacup, Jessy realized. Granted, Hale was a touch different, fanatically tidy, but he wouldn't pick on helpless kids. She laughed at herself. The culprits bothering these Salonika kids were probably other kids who just needed to be told a thing or two about decency.

Lucian was defensive, "What's so funny?"

Jessy shook her head. "Never mind. If I told you, you'd cart me off to the looney bin. For a second I thought—no, it was a stupid notion, honestly. But you and the younger kids will get to stay in Ardensville for as long as you want—your whole lives if you want to. I don't know how yet, but Lucian, I'll try to help you."

Chapter 7

JESSY DECIDED she had to talk to Lombard Hale, appointment or not. With no police force in town, the mayor had to stop the hoodlums from bothering the Salonikas. Hadn't Mr. Hale told her, earlier, to bring her problems to him? She'd go straight to his house, and he would have to make time for her. She mustn't lose her nerve, though.

Late on Tuesday, at the Hale mansion, Anna Cora answered Jessy's knock. "You remember me, don't you?" Jessy asked her with a smile. "I'm Jessy Faber, Central. Anna Cora, is your father in? He didn't know I was coming, but I have to see him."

Anna Cora Hale looked at Jessy shyly for a long moment. "Miss Jessy Faber? You want to see father?" She stepped back. A tiny smile gave a hint of prettiness to her otherwise plain features. "Daddy is in his study. Come with me." Anna darted away, almost ghostlike in her loose, cream-colored dress.

Jessy followed through magnificent rooms, until finally, Anna

Cora halted in front of double doors in a long hallway. The girl knocked, opened the doors and motioned Jessy to go in. "Thank y—" Jessy tried to say but Anna Cora was already disappearing back the way they'd come.

She took a deep breath and went in. It was a big, rich room. Dark, shiny wood tables, maroon upholstered sofas and chairs, glowing lamplight. From behind his desk Lombard Hale swung toward her, his hands outstretched. "Miss Faber! How nice of you to visit. Anna Cora, dear," he called out, "now don't run off!" He trotted out, down the hall, then returned, shrugging.

"She's gone back to her dolls, no doubt. My Annie is an angel," he said, "and I'd like you two sweet girls to get better acquainted. Only friend Annie has is—is that common laborer, Cecil Kinglake." He frowned, then brightened slightly, "And of course, she has Mrs. Pierce, Wilford's wife, who buys her dresses. Ah, well. Come sit down my dear. Tell me what brings you here?"

Lombard Hale's gracious manners threw Jessy off. He was powerful. Important. She sat stiffly in the chair he gave her, the fingers of one hand tightly pinched in the other. "Mr. Hale," she managed to say through her dry throat, "I would like to talk to you about something that has me very worried, a family in trouble."

"Of course, of course," he said. He picked up his chair in back of his desk and brought it closer to her. "Don't worry, dear. Whatever it is we'll take care of it. You have my word."

"Good!" Jessy sighed. "It's the Salonikas, Mr. Hale, the children who live in the church woods on Liberty Street. I know this sounds ridiculous, sir, but someone has been giving them no end of trouble, being downright cruel, trying to get them to leave town, we think. It must be hoodlums, throwing rocks, setting fire to their—" The change Jessy saw come to Hale's expression stopped her. The warm smile vanished, the expression in his eyes was flat and cold.

"They aren't hurting a soul," Jessy ventured to go on, after a moment. "They are good children who only want to live, go to school—"

"Aliens!" Hale chopped her off. "Human garbage, Miss Faber!"

Jessy recoiled as if he had slapped her. She'd thought, earlier, that Hale might feel this way, yet she wasn't ready to hear it. "You can't mean it," she choked out, "you can't. They aren't hurting you, they aren't a bother to anyone."

Amazingly, Lombard's smile returned. "You are too young to understand, my child," he told her. "It is plain to see you do not know what is going on in this country. Foreign trash has washed up on our shores, to breed like lice in America." He leaned toward her. "We can't let it continue, dear. Catholics, Jews, these aliens, must not be allowed to stay; they will take over. Take over our beloved country. We want our beautiful land to be pure, don't we, pure, white, all-American? Do you see?" His voice was soft, his expression fatherly-mild once more.

"No, I don't see." Where the courage to talk back came from, Jessy didn't know. She hurried on, because Hale was frowning again. "Your people were aliens in this land at one time, Mr. Hale. Yours, mine, just about everybody's ancestors came to America from somewhere else." Her heart drummed so furiously in her ears, Jessy could scarcely hear her own voice. "The Indian is the only pure American. He was here first. And he isn't white. His skin is red."

Hale protested, "That was so long ago it no longer matters. This is my town. My people founded it, laid out the very streets, built the first business establishments, they incorporated it and named it for my mother's people, *Arden's*—ville. This is a fine town because I and my people have made it that way. Girl, this town is—is my heart."

"All—all right!" Jessy cried, her hands waved wildly of their own accord. "Your family built the town, and Ardensville is a beautiful place. I wouldn't claim anything else. But a small family of children who happen to be very poor, have skin darker than ours, and who have come very far from a different country, isn't going to change the town."

He stood up, shaking his head. "Miss Faber, you are blind. Others like them will come. The town will be ruined. We have to prevent that. I have friends in high places," he warned, "who share my view. Besides, those urchins are trespassers, breaking the law. I have written several letters to a Mrs. Pickering in Denver who owns the piece of property those dirty urchins are camped on. She and her husband bought the land after a heavy snow caved in the church roof; termites had eaten into the wood of the building. The congregation decided to build elsewhere and they salvaged the parsonage, took it with them. The Pickerings bought the land, thinking to come here themselves. But they never did. Never even saw the place, I think. But I'm sure she wouldn't want it lived in by a bunch of riffraff. I understand she is ill. Her son is living in Europe. When Mrs. Pickering recovers, I know she will want the children removed. There are going to be some changes in Ardensville. Quite a few citizens agree that—" he stopped abruptly, with a look that indicated he'd almost said something he didn't want known.

What was the use, anyway? Jessy wondered. Lombard Hale had all but admitted that he was behind the harassment of the Salonika children, he and others. As strong as the mayor's hate was, Lucian's letter of permission would be as useful as a bit of ash. The man would probably go to any end to see them thrown out. But what could she do? Jessy stood up to leave and found that her knees were wobbly. Still, she raked up courage for a parting remark. "We don't agree about anything, Mr. Hale," she said, "and I doubt if we ever will."

Turning, Jessy saw that Anna Cora waited by the door with a worried frown. Jessy tried to smile reassurance. "Anna Cora," she whispered, "would you show me out?"

Anna Cora nodded, a child's look of sympathy on her face.

"Give what I said a lot of thought, Miss Faber," Hale shouted after them. "You'll know then, dear, that I am right." She heard him chuckle. He added, "A farm girl ought to know that a few bad apples will spoil the whole barrel."

Jessy bit her tongue. The Salonikas were human beings, not apples, or candy wrappers, for heaven's sake! Tears of anger and frustration blurred her eyes as she stumbled along the carpet that ran down the middle of the hallway.

"Thank you," Jessy murmured to Anna Cora at the door. She hurried outside and took gulps of the cool night air in a vain attempt to calm herself.

Back in her room, Jessy sat on the bed and cuddled Cowboy to her, crying. "I'm such a bungler," she whispered, "I'm not doing any better here in Ardensville than at home. I want to do the proper thing for those kids. I do. But what?" Hale was *wrong*. He didn't *own* the town. The people here didn't belong to him. What right did he have to say this person may stay, that person can't? Yet she knew that most everyone looked up to the mayor. Mr. Hale had a large and loyal following.

A day or two later Jessy decided that the town meeting might be the answer. Ardensville had a town meeting once each month. It always drew a large crowd, she'd heard. The month before, she had made her first announcement about it. She hadn't gone to that one, but she now decided she would go to the next and mention the children. It would take gumption, and it would be hard to make a complaint in front of the whole town. But could she stand by and let this rotten treatment of innocent kids go on?

Maybe others would speak up, after her. There surely ought to be some people on her side. With that help, maybe something could be done. She wasn't sure, though—

On her free Sunday, two days before the Tuesday night town meeting, Jessy decided she had to get away. She hadn't been on a horse since coming to Ardensville; she'd rent a saddle horse at the livery and ride as far as she could go, away from town. The country would be peaceful, her mind could work better there. And she'd plan what she'd say, word for word, at the town meeting.

While she was gone, she wouldn't even have to worry that there would be trouble at the switchboard because of Gussie's drinking; she'd stopped. The episode—tangling the switchboard—had been a kind of grand finale. Right about then, a widower had taken up residence at Lilli's boarding house, and he and Gussie had taken a real shine to one another. She probably didn't need her "tonic" because she wasn't so lonely anymore.

ONCE JESSY'S MIND was made up to go on the outing, she could hardly wait. On Sunday she dressed in loden green slacks, a tan blouse and a light sweater. She made a sandwich and apple lunch to take along, and rented a saddle horse from the livery. Joe Cooke, at his shoeshine stand, spotted her as she was riding away from the stable toward the northwest road out of town. "You make a pretty picture, Miss Central," he called out to her. "You and that little chestnut mare got hair 'bout the same color."

Jessy threaded the fingers of her free hand through the horse's coarse mane, and laughed. "I think you're right; we match," she told Joe.

An hour and more later, with the town and small farms well behind her, Jessy began to feel better than she had in some time. There wasn't a lot to pleasure the eye, really, she decided as she rode, just rolling grassland dotted here and there with grazing cattle. Once in a while a tall windmill and tank broke the unvarying skyline. Closer to view were even less interesting objects, like the horned skull of a cow hooked on a barbed wire fence. It was the *change* of scene she liked so much, Jessy decided.

When the sun was directly overhead Jessy rode into a sunken area in the land, a kind of valley broken by a sluggish, brush-lined creek. Beside the creek would be a good place to spread her blanket for her picnic, she decided. At the roadside, Jessy tied the mare to the barbed wire fence, slipped through the wires, and looked for cattle. None in sight. She didn't want to meet an ornery range bull, that was for sure.

In the meager shade of a prickly bush, Jessy spread the blanket and sat down. She ate slowly and watched dragonflies play tag on the surface of the brown water.

Finished eating, she took off her shoes and stockings and rolled up the legs of her slacks. The ground was hot under her bare feet. Jessy minced on tiptoe to the creek, then splashed into the thick warm water, laughing out loud like a little girl. Why hadn't she brought a fishpole?

Wishing she didn't have to, Jessy finally climbed out of the creek. As she looked down at her feet, a sickening horror swept through her. Several ugly black leeches, *bloodsuckers*, had fastened themselves onto her white skin. "Shoot!" she said out loud. Why did this have to happen? Jessy crawled awkwardly on hands and knees across the burning ground to her blanket; she sat down cross-legged and pulled her feet up close so she could examine them.

Taking hold of one of the ugly black worms, she tried to pull it free. Useless. The leech was hooked tight. Tears stung her eyes as she squeezed her flesh hard about the leech in an effort to loosen its mouth.

"Hup. Hold on, that ain't how to do it." A deep voice broke the afternoon stillness above her. Jessy jerked about, startled, to see a man, possibly in his mid-twenties, striding down the bank toward her. She took in his sweat-stained, wide-brimmed hat, dark blue shirt with a tobacco tag hanging out of the pocket, worn Levis, and scarred boots—a cowboy. Probably come to tell her she was trespassing, Jessy decided, and of course she was.

Chapter 8

JESSY MOVED BACK a bit when the cowboy knelt beside her. His face looked familiar, somehow. "We'll put a little heat on the leeches," he explained, lighting a match with a flick of his thumbnail. "That will move 'em out. Sit quiet now, Miss," he told her. "I'm gonna hold this match as close as I can to the bugger, but I don't want to burn you."

She didn't know what to say. This stranger took helping her for granted. "All—all right," she mumbled.

"Hurt?" he wanted to know. He held the flaming match away from the leech for a second. "Don't want to burn you."

Jessy shook her head quickly. "You—you didn't burn me. No more than the ground did, walking barefoot. It's all right. I hate the awful things. I tried but I couldn't get them out."

The cowboy nodded and brought his match close to the leech again. "If it gets too hot, tell me." Jessy gave a little motion with her hand, bit her lip, but said nothing aloud. His shoulder was so broad she couldn't see around it, so she gave up trying to watch the procedure. Jessamyn closed her eyes. "There." She heard his deep murmur a while later. "That one's out. Now it's this one's turn."

In another moment Jessy opened her eyes and found the cowboy's own blue eyes looking closely at her. He grinned sheepishly. "Pardon me for starin'. I keep thinkin' I've seen you somewhere before."

"Me, too." Jessy nodded shyly, "I mean, I thought that I'd seen you before, too. But I can't think where." It was sliding about on the edges of her mind, and Jessy was about to remember, when the cowboy rocked back on his heels and slapped his thigh.

"Mandy's!" they said at the same time.

"Couple months ago," he chuckled. "It was in Mandy's all right, I was just heading into the cafe with my boss, and you were coming out."

"Just a little over a month ago," Jessy corrected, surprised that he would remember at all, and pleased. "That was my first day in Ardensville, and at the time I hardly knew if I was coming or going." Jessy smiled at him, then gasped suddenly as the match touched her bare foot. "Oww!"

"I'm sorry!" He frowned and reached for her hand. "Burned you anyways. I'm a durn clumsy fool. Wasn't paying attention."

Jessy shook her head. "It wasn't anything. Just scared me a minute, it didn't really hurt." She looked at her hand swallowed inside his and felt odd—giddy. She pulled her hand free. "Are—you about finished?"

"One more of the son-of-a-guns, and we're done," he answered. Over his shoulder he mumbled, "My name is Hatcher Elroy. Hatch, to most folks."

"I'm Jessamyn Faber—and I like people to call me Jessy. I live in town, Ardensville—I'm the new telephone operator there. This is my day off, things were going so nice till I stopped wading and saw I'd gotten these awful bloodsuckers hooked into my feet."

She sighed. "I should have known better, should have known leeches might be in muddy water like this."

Later, getting to his feet, Hatch Elroy joked, "You still got a few pints of blood they didn't get, I reckon." When he saw Jessy struggle to get up, his hand came down quick to grasp her elbow and help.

As soon as she was standing, Jessy realized that her feet were still bare, that she had forgotten to put her shoes and stockings on. She sat down again, embarrassed. What on earth was the matter with her today! "My shoes," she mumbled crazily. When she looked up, she saw the cowboy still standing there. Why didn't he go on about his business? An audience to her foolishness she didn't need.

In another minute her things were in her arms, and Jessy was ready to leave. Without a glance, or further word to the cowboy, she started toward her horse. The man followed her! With no small amount of starch in her voice, Jessy said to him, "Thank you, Mr. Elroy. I'm quite all right now. I can manage by myself."

Hatch Elroy gave her a puzzled look but didn't break his stride. Jessy saw then why he kept coming. A black horse with white stockings was ground-reined out at the road beside her chestnut mare. Color rose in Jessy's cheeks. How had she expected the poor man to get to his horse, anyway, fly? She *was* behaving like a perfect idiot and couldn't seem to stop!

Hatch Elroy said, as though he could read her mind, "I'd take another path, but there ain't none."

Finally, overcome with the silliness of it all, Jessy laughed, nearly dropping her blanket and picnic basket. When she looked at Hatch Elroy, she saw him whopping his leg with his stetson, laughing, too. Her breath caught raggedly.

Trying to restrain her giggles, Jessy slipped through the strands of barbed wire as Hatch held them wide apart for her.

She mounted her horse and relaxed in the saddle. With her glance pinned on Hatch Elroy's curly brown hair—she couldn't for anything look into those blue eyes—Jessy asked, "Do you mind that I trespassed on your ranch?"

Hatch climbed onto his horse and held the reins loose. "I'm just foreman of the Bar M," he told Jessy. "But old Tom Moorehouse, he wouldn't mind, either." He grinned teasingly at her. "Just as long as you leave his cows be and only take leeches out of his crick." He tipped his hat to her, bringing again to mind the first time she'd seen him at Mandy's.

"Is this good-bye or are you ridin' on my way?" he wanted to know.

She shook her head. "It's time I got back to town. My cat—" Until this second she hadn't remembered she'd named the kitten for this cowboy. She shrugged. "Thanks again for getting those nasty things off my feet." When Jessy lifted her glance to meet his with a smile, her heart did flipflops. She was glad no one but herself knew it.

"S'long. Nice meetin' you, Jessamyn." He waved. "Jessy." He drew his horse around and cantered away from her.

Jessy turned her own horse back toward town, wondering at her feelings. She didn't want him to go! Which was silly. Hatch Elroy was a perfect stranger. *Jessamyn Faber, don't you look back at him, don't you dare*, she warned herself. She looked back, finally, but by then he was no more than a speck on the skyline.

TWO NIGHTS LATER, Lombard Hale didn't look surprised or annoyed that Jessy had come to the town meeting. His greeting was a frothy rich as sweetened whipped cream; coming as it did after their recent set-to, it made Jessy feel ill. As soon as she could, she moved away from him and threaded her way through the gathering crowd, saying hello to those townspeople she knew by sight.

She was *here*. Although she wasn't exactly sure what she should say, Jessy wasn't worried. After Sunday, getting away, meeting the cowboy, she felt different. She felt relaxed, somehow more sure of herself. After tonight, the Salonika children could stay in Ardensville without trouble, she hoped. And she would be able to turn her mind to other things. Hatcher Elroy, maybe.

The meeting was about to start. Six council members—Mr. Pierce and the mayor, Lombard Hale, among them—sat behind a long table facing the main crowd. Jessy took a chair near the center aisle so she could stand up easily when her chance came. She understood that after the most pressing town affairs had been covered, the meeting would be thrown open to hear problems from the townspeople.

Jessy sat back, half-listening to debate about need for a new city cistern, board sidewalks that needed repair, and a discussion of a budget for the Ardensville Public School. In those two hours her mind came clear as to what she wanted to say about the Salonikas: *They were innocent kids being tormented for no good reason. They needed protection. A fire was a serious threat. The children had rights. Finally, the person or persons responsible must be made to stop.*

Finally, it was time for the townspeople to air their troubles. Her mind dulled by boredom, Jessy was slow to react. Before she could get to her feet, two men were up and hard into an argument about ownership of a fence that divided their individual properties. The main problem seemed to be who was responsible for upkeep. Each of the men "remembered for a fact" who built the fence and when, but their facts were in sharp disagreement.

It was decided after long argument that the matter would have to be put off until the mayor could check court records where true ownership might be legally documented.

When the men sat back down, grumbling, Jessy got to her feet. She drew a deep breath and plunged, "Ladies and gentlemen, Mr. Mayor, councilmen, there are some children in this town who—" she broke off, dumbfounded, when Lombard Hale got to his feet fast and began speaking as though he were unaware that she'd spoken first.

"We have a serious matter here that I should have brought up earlier," he announced. "We must deal with this, folks, right away before it gets worse." He wagged his head and brought forth a newspaper, which he waved back and forth. "This is terrible," he said, "what this writer is up to. Disgusting. I'm sure most of you know what I am talking about."

She didn't. Jessy sat down slowly, her chin lifted in shaky anger that he'd stopped her, but curious, too. For some reason, she felt uneasy.

Someone asked, "What's in that newspaper, Mayor?"

"Stories," Hale replied, his voice heavy. "Untrue stories about our fair town and its good citizens. I don't mind saying, I am shocked! And the writer is too cowardly to use her own name. She signs this fabricated nonsense, *Anona Missee.*"

"Anonymous," someone repeated in a whisper.

"That's the *Denver Community Herald* you got there," a man in the audience declared suddenly, "an' you're talking about that serial they're running, 'Nora's Neighbors.'"

The owner of the livery stable spoke up then. "They've been writing about *us*? I wondered why that Nora story about the stable failin' sounded familiar." The man thundered indignantly, "It's them newfangled automobiles that's ruinin' me, but my money losses ain't nobody's business but mine!"

A woman on the far side of the room from Jessy stood up. She looked pale and close to fainting. "Then that means—the shotgun wedding story was about my—my daughter...." She slumped back into her chair.

"I thought that was your girl, Mabel, when I read it," a second woman said. "The names was different in the story, but the details was all the same. I recognized your Mabel right off."

What on earth were they talking about? Jessy wondered. The whole thing sounded idiotic. She'd never heard of "Nora's Neighbors" before tonight. Except for Ardensville's *Review Times*, she hardly ever looked at a newspaper. She wished they could get to things that mattered, like the Salonika children.

"I ain't seen that newspaper," someone said. "What's them stories like, and how can they get by with it? Ain't this slander?"

"The *Denver Community Herald* refers to the serial as fiction." Hale scoffed. "They insist the stories are made up and have no connection with actual persons. Do they really think we are fooled?" He began to shout, "This writer, without a care for Ardensville folks' right to privacy, is exploiting our good peoples' personal affairs, embroidering the tales just enough so she can call them made-up fiction."

Jessy winced as a man close to her shouted hoarsely, "Well, let's do something about it!"

An angry buzz rose in the room. Jessy looked about her with worry. She faced the front when she heard someone ask, "Who do you think's writing about us, Mayor?"

The room noise softened. Mr. Hale cleared his throat. "We must be careful. Mustn't jump to false conclusions. Considering the situation, I believe it is a newcomer to our fair town. Someone who hasn't lived here long enough to care, to want what is best for all of us, for Ardensville!" He looked directly into the faces before him. "On the other hand, this new arrival would have to be in a position to know everything that goes on in Ardensville."

Every pair of eyes in the room, it seemed, turned to her. The silence was thick with threat, with feeling. Not her! They couldn't mean this. Jessy began to laugh from nerves. And because it was funny. She covered her mouth to try and smother her giggles that wouldn't stop bubbling up.

She laughed alone.

Chapter 9

IT'S CENTRAL WRITIN' this stuff!" a voice stormed. "Makin' fools of us all. She knows everything, listening in on our calls. Look at her laugh. And what do we know about her? Nothing! We lettin' her get by with using us?"

Another voice conjectured, "She probably come here just to make money for herself writing stories about what she heard."

Ready to burst with combined laughter and tears, Jessy somehow got to her feet. "Please... please, listen to me," she said softly, trying to keep her face straight. They quieted to hear her. "I am not this writer—this Nora, or Anona Missee, or whatever it is you're saying. I have never set eyes on the newspaper. Tonight is the first I've heard about these stories, truly."

"If it ain't you, Central, who is it? Nobody can know as much about all of us as you do."

"How should I know who wrote the stories?" Jessy cried. She clasped her trembling hands together. "I don't know everybody's business, either. Wait a minute," she pleaded when a grumbling arose, "you know one another's affairs as much or more than I do. I could point to quite a few people in this room whom I have warned more than once about listening in on other's calls, weakening the circuits. Isn't that right?"

She shivered as the venom in expressions turned her way. White-knuckled, she held onto the back of the chair in front of her. "If—if you want to know who the writer is, why doesn't someone, the mayor maybe, write to the newspaper? They might not tell you who it is, b-but I'm sure they'll gladly tell you it's not me. That can be proven. Now," she gulped, "about something else—"

In that second Lombard Hale's gavel came up and then banged down on the front table. "Meeting adjourned," he declared. "We've already gone long past our time for adjournment."

Jessy stared at him in disbelief. People, still in heated discussion of the "Nora" stories, filed toward the door. He couldn't have planned this ahead of time to keep her from talking about Lucian and the children. He couldn't have known she would be here tonight, even. Maybe Hale had meant to bring up the Nora stories all along. Then, seeing her here and guessing why, he'd twisted the situation to his own advantage.

The satisfied smile on Lombard Hale's face as he gathered his papers to go told Jessy her guess was close enough. What was the use? Her hands slipped from the chair in front of her. How could he do this, be so unfair?

Jessy's feelings of futility and upset hung on for days. Yet, visiting the Salonika children, she was told that nothing bad had happened for weeks. "We wouldn't run, so they decided to give up," Lucian insisted. "We don't care if the troublemakers don't have to pay for what they did, if they just leave us alone, now. It isn't your fight, anyway, Jessamyn," he told her. "Put it out of your head."

She was more than willing to do just that. "Are you sure everything is all right?" she asked, feeling like a mountain had been moved from her shoulders.

"Fine. There aren't as many odd jobs for me right now, but that will pass. Nobody is bothering us. It's over, Jessy."

Over. Jessy hoped it was true.

ON A CRISP FALL DAY as Jessy was leaving the telephone office for her noon meal, she almost collided with Lilli Miller coming to meet her. "Let's go to Mandy's," Lilli cried, "I have the best news, kid!"

Lilli's high spirits were catching. Jessy laughed and followed along. At Mandy's, Lilli carefully laid a magazine on the table. Jessy looked, curious and saw that it was a recent issue of a new true love magazine. "Open it," Lilli commanded, "page nineteen." Her hazel eyes glowed. She propped her chin in her hand and watched as Jessy flipped the pages. "That one!" Lilli pointed, "that story called, 'He Loved Me Too Much.' What do you think?"

Jessy lowered her eyes to read. After a few paragraphs, she felt a warmth crawling up her throat. Carefully, she put the magazine down. "The story sounds—uh, spicy, Lilli. But I'm sure it is good, if you think so."

Lilli's small braid-crowned head lifted proudly. "I wrote it."

"You what?" Jessy whispered. "Lilli, you wrote that story?"

"Oh, yes, I did. And I never had so much fun in my life." She giggled. "Look, Jessy, it—it might not be your kind of story. But will you read it, the whole story, and tell me your honest opinion of it? It would mean a lot to me."

"I—I don't know…. Oh, sure I will." Jessy grinned and studied Lilli's flushed face. "So you're a writer, Lilli? In all our talks you didn't mention that."

"I've felt all my life that I am a writer, kid. But I didn't want anyone to know until I could prove it, be published."

"Lil, what do you know about Anona Missee?"

Lilli looked surprised, "You read 'Nora's Neighbors?'"

"No." Jessy shook her head. "I've never seen the newspaper the serial is in." In a light tone she went on to tell how the stories had gotten her into hot water at the town meeting; that she had been accused of being the anonymous collector and writer of Ardensville's deepest secrets.

"How unfair of them to say it was you," Lilli declared. She dimpled. "They ought to give credit where credit is due." An expression of vague regret showed fleetingly in her face. "Look, kid, I'm not admitting a thing, you understand, but I don't think you'll have to worry about those newspaper stories anymore. The last installment ran a week ago. Postage to Denver every week adds up." Her hand strayed to the magazine, and she smoothed it, "The author, I understand, is going on to more profitable writing."

Jessy read Lilli's love story in bed that night. She had trouble finding it believable. The beautiful housewife the story was about sinned and suffered over much, it seemed to her. But she did like the way Lilli's words kind of dazzled and danced in her mind, or off the tongue when she read sentences aloud. She'd be glad to tell Lilli that, Jessy decided. She snuggled deeper under the covers.

Nothing like the stuff in Lilli's story had ever happened to her, but long ago Farley had kissed her a few times. Jessy raised her head and told the kitten lying on top of the quilt, warming her toes, "Let's go to sleep. We don't want to keep thinking about Farley, do we? Not the other one, either," she said. "He doesn't know we're alive, kitty-cat." Jessy smothered a yawn. Cowboy, looking back at her, yawned, too.

Jessy smiled and lay back, staring at the ceiling. She'd seen Hatcher Elroy early in the evening not many days ago, as she was taking a minute from the board to let Cowboy into the telephone office. Hatch saw her, too, as he came out of Mandy's, across the street. For a second he acted as if he was coming over to talk to her. Then an older rancher, waiting in a truck, yelled at Hatch to hurry, somebody named Etta would be mad if they didn't "hit the road."

She couldn't understand it; from that night on, a kind of warm miserableness, had bothered her. Made her feel restless, dreamy.

Which was probably why, Jessy decided later, she didn't pay more attention when the rash of small emergencies started to come through her switchboard. A rock was thrown through the window of Burmann's Department Store. At first Mr. Burmann asked to be connected with the police at Macloud, then he changed his mind. He wanted the hardware store instead. So he could just order a window and forget the matter, he told Jessy.

One day, the two youngest of the large McGuire clan vanished. With a public announcement, Jessy asked for search parties, asked people to keep a lookout. Mysteriously, without explanation, the tots were found unharmed twelve hours afterward, sitting on their own front porch.

Later, Jessy began to wonder again. The broken window wasn't so bad, just costly, but the babies—they shouldn't just disappear, be gone for so long, then turn up with no explanation. It brought to mind again the Salonika fire, the heckling. Why were these things happening? To frighten people, make them leave, was the only answer. *It wasn't over.*

These days Lucian's problem was finding enough odd jobs to keep food on the table. She had found out that he was suddenly being treated like a nuisance by people who'd earlier given him work. As though someone had passed an order: starve the Salonikas out.

For hours at a time, Jessy would stare at the switchboard in front of her, working automatically as her mind tried to figure it all out. She could come up with no answers.

She tried to keep her mind on her job. And she did almost always have answers to the questions people asked. "Number please?… What is playing at the ORPHEUM? Clara Bow, in *Down to the Sea In Ships*…. You're welcome." She plugged into another jack. "How is Grandpa Ellis this afternoon? Doctor says he is better. Lots. He's taking soup," Jessy informed the fifth such caller.

Leaving work for supper one night, she stopped on the sidewalk as her problem finally came together. There was a thread, she realized. A *thread*. The emergencies, the happenings, had struck people who were—different. Mr. Burmann, a Jew. The McGuire family, Irish—Catholic. Lucian, Christ and Althea and little Delphine—were Greek, dark-skinned, and they dressed differently and lived a stray-cat kind of way.

Goosebumps prickled along Jessy's arms. Blind. She was blind not to have seen it long before this. In his own words Lombard Hale had told her how he felt about foreigners and Catholics and Jews. *Trash*, his word. *They didn't belong in his town.* Clutter.

Hale, maybe others, too, were working to drive some people from Ardensville.

She wanted to know what Lilli thought and decided to skip supper.

In Lilli's parlor, Jessy felt better, spilling what was on her mind. But Lilli looked dreadfully sober, for her. "That's how it looks to me," Jessy finished. "Hale alone or maybe there's others, too, are hounding the few families in Ardensville who are a bit different. I'm sorry to tell you something so ugly and unbelievable, Lilli."

Lilli barely nodded. "Tell me," Jessy begged, "what do you think, Lilli?"

"The Invisible Empire." Her tone was so flat and lifeless, it was hard for Jessy to hear her. The *KKK*."

"You idiot!" Jessy laughed. "The Ku Klux Klan? Oh, Lilli, that's silly. Not in Ardensville, Kansas. This isn't Kansas City, or Atlanta, for goodness sake."

Lilli continued to look grave. "I'm not joking, kid. I mean it. This stuff you told me, about the Greek kids and Isaac Burmann and the McGuires. I didn't think much about it when those things happened, either. But now that you've added it up—" She bit her lip. "Do you read the papers, Jess?"

She shook her head. "I don't, hardly ever, except the little local paper. My problem is, I hear so much 'news' through my switchboard, it's about all I can stand."

Lilli rubbed her arms and answered, "It may be that the Ku Kluxers haven't actually grouped in Ardensville, but the Klan could have a scattering of believers here. Unless there are things—parades, cross burnings—out in the open, it could be here and we wouldn't know. Anyway, somebody is borrowing Klan tactics, I think. Say Lombard Hale—"

"I thought the Ku Klux Klan bothered Negroes, down South? That it happened a long time ago and was all over with?"

Lilli was patient. "The Klan started up again not long ago, kid. The country is changing. A lot of people are scared, Jessy, of bad times. They think that blacks, and foreigners coming here, will take their jobs. Drinking and gambling has picked up, and that worries people, too. They want their America pure. And pure to them is white, Protestant."

It was like an echo of Hale's words. Jessy said, "It sounds so narrow-minded, closed."

"Remember your history books, kid? Worry and fear has been known to bring out the worst in the best of people." Lilli shrugged. "Love and tolerance seems to go out the window when people get afraid."

"I think—I hope, you're wrong, Lilli. About the Klan being here," Jessy had to tell her. "What you say might be true in big cities. But in Kansas? In Ardensville? And what about Joe Cooke, the bootblack? Nobody bothers him."

Lilli's eyes on her were keen. "Joe and his sons keep pretty much to themselves. He's probably the one person in town who wouldn't ring Central for help. Now that I remember—" Lilli sat up. "There is something. I didn't think about the Klan in connection with it, before. Joe's been wanting to buy the livery stable and blacksmith shop. Legal red-tape has kept him from doing it."

"With Lombard Hale holding the red-tape?" Jessy sighed. "Who else?"

NO MORE REAL EMERGENCIES came through the switch-board in the next few weeks, and Jessy took heart. Mrs. McGuire seemed to be her own happy self again, although she was never seen without her two youngest in tow. Mr. Burmann's new window was larger and better than the old one.

Best of all, when she visited the Salonikas, Lucian was seldom home. Lilli redoing several rooms at her boarding house, was keeping Luc busy doing carpentry. The other three were going to school, had new school clothes, books, and tablets.

Jessy wanted to believe nothing more would happen, but deep inside she couldn't be sure.

Chapter 10

ON A COLD NOVEMBER NIGHT, Jessy and Lilli sat in Lilli's cozy kitchen sharing a late supper Lilli had fixed. "I'm sorry, Lilli, my mind keeps wandering. What were you saying?" Jessy asked. Actually, she knew full well what Lilli had been asking her. She really didn't want to talk about Joe Cooke's troubles, or anybody else's.

"I said, 'Will you go?' This meeting is for Joe. He's trying again to buy the livery and blacksmith shop. I was telling you, he wants it not so much to shoe horses as to do metal repair jobs and stuff."

"Well." Jessy sighed. "If he has the money and wants to buy the shop, what's stopping him?" She tasted a forkful of apple pie. "M-mm, this is good! You don't look like a cook, Lilli, but you are." Lilli wasn't pleased that she had changed the subject. So Jessy gave in and asked further, "Why does there have to be a meeting?"

"You still aren't reading the papers, are you, kid?" Lilli said. "Even the local rag!" When Jessy shook her head, Lilli sighed patiently. "A fellow named Cameron owns the livery now. But he has it up for sale. Joe has the money to buy it. He's made several offers, but Cameron keeps turning him down. For once, Joe Cooke lost his temper, I guess, and there was an argument. The mayor is going to hold court tonight to find out who is guilty of what. It's an open meeting, anyone can go. I want to be there to put in a good word for Joe Cooke if there's a chance. You want to, too, don't you, Jess?"

"I went to one town meeting," Jessy reminded her. "It turned out to be a sideshow with me in the middle. No, I don't want to go. That's my only week-night off, and I have some mending to do, buttons and such. I haven't bought a new dress since I came here and all my things—"

"Jessy, I don't understand you. Yes"—Lilli sat back in her chair—"on the other hand maybe I do. You know what's going to happen to Joe. You know Hale will have his way, that he and others, white robes on or not, will massacre Joe Cooke's dream. You don't want to see it."

Jessy's face was hot. If she could just make clear *her* side. "Lilli, listen. I wanted to help the Salonika kids, but I thought that that was all there was. If it's bigger, I don't want to be *in* it."

"You admit then, that there is something rotten going on in Ardensville? Well, hon, we can't just hold our noses and look the other way," Lilli told her. "Now you make me wonder—were you using those Salonika kids? Taking on their troubles so you wouldn't have to face your own—whatever it is from your past you've been trying to block out?"

Lilli might as well have slapped her. Tears stung Jessy's eyes. Was Lilli right? "I hate town meetings, I hate politics," she whispered. "I don't like Lombard Hale, that's all."

"You're stalling," Lilli accused softly. Her grin was kind, affectionate. "Jessy, this isn't really you."

"Oh, Lilli. All right. I will go with you. But I won't like it. And how come Lombard Hale can hold a real court?"

"Besides being mayor, he is a licensed notary public Justice of the Peace." Lilli nodded. "If we could find some proper beaus to marry, Hale could even tie the knots for us, Jess."

Lilli's joke eased the tension between them, but only a little.

THE TOWN HALL WAS CROWDED for the special meeting. Jessy sat stiffly beside Lilli. She should have come up with a better reason to come. If it got to shouting, trouble—she was going to leave. No matter what Lilli thought.

Jessy couldn't shake off her feeling of dread, and she was only partly aware of proceedings as the meeting ran on and on. At last, Mr. Cameron and Joe Cooke were found equally guilty of disturbing the peace. Each was charged a small fine. There was no mention of the livery sale. Jessy let out a satisfied sigh. They could go now.

"The real issue here is being swept right under the rug." Jessy looked and saw a woman, Mandy Phillips, on her feet, speaking. "Joe has rights," Mandy said. "He wants to buy a business of his own, the livery and blacksmith shop, but he's being blocked from doing it. Most of you know it, too. If it's because he's black, that's stupid. A black man ought to be able to own his own business the same as me, or anybody else. As an American citizen, he has a right."

Lilli was gleeful. "Well said," she whispered, "good for Mandy."

Jessy could feel it coming now. *Trouble.*

Someone in back shouted hoarsely, "A right to take over, you mean? You let one black in, and the next thing you know a whole passel of 'em will be running the town."

Lombard Hale looked pleased at that. He tapped his gavel half-heartedly. "Let's have order."

"Joe is a good man." Jessy saw that it was Mr. McGuire, square-shouldered, in a worn suit, speaking. His face showed fear, but he continued. "Joe earned his money the hard way. He and his boys have lived down to the bone in order to save nickels and dimes so he could—"

"You don't get that much money shinin' shoes," an angry voice interrupted, "not enough to buy a livery stable. Nosirree! If a darky's got cash like that, where'd he get it? That's what I'd like to know."

Jessy wanted to cover her ears. She started to rise, but Lilli caught her arm. "Don't go, it will be all right, Jessy. We can't walk out. We care, don't we?"

Jessy shook her head, then nodded. She cared. But her tongue felt thick, her throat dry. She sat down uncertainly. The meeting was supposed to be over, wasn't it? Why couldn't they leave?

Finally, the heated voices and the shuffling and thumping quieted. Lombard Hale looked out over his audience with good-natured authority. He spoke, his voice tinged with regret, "I didn't want to bring this up, but I have no choice. Everyone must understand that no injustice has been served on Joe here. Quite the opposite as a matter of fact. I have had occasion to look into Joe's background—" Jessy saw Joe stiffen and dart a closer look at Lombard Hale.

"Joe was a schoolteacher at one time, in the Ozarks," Hale said. "There was a school outing, a field trip, I believe it is called." He cleared his throat and lowered his voice, "A little girl—died on that field trip." The room went still.

Joe stood up. Holding his hat to his chest, he faced Lombard Hale. "Mr. Mayor, sir," he said in a trembling voice, "it was an accident. I was cleared."

The mayor nodded. "Yes, I know. The children at first said the little *white* girl in your school fell over the cliff accidentally. But others maintain she—was trying to get away from you."

"I was trying to help her," Joe insisted. "The children know.

They saw Mary slip and fall. They know I went to help her, but the ground caved from under her before I could catch hold of her hand. I was cleared," he said again.

"Joe, we've gone over that," Hale reproved him. "Now I want you to tell the folks why you didn't stay on in that town, teaching your little school? There must be a reason? Joe?"

A long silence followed. Joe answered finally, his voice breaking, "There was—there was—rope talk. Some didn't want to believe the truth. My—my wife died. Her heart gave out, living so scared—I left."

"You left." Lombard Hale repeated. "You bummed around the country, I understand. Finally, you came to our good town. Although you weren't wanted where you came from, we let you stay in our midst, we gave you work as a bootblack. What more do you want, Joe? We made you welcome."

"I didn't do anything wrong," Joe protested. "All I want is—"

"Joe," Hale interrupted, "the matter is settled. You know your place." He banged the gavel. "This meeting is adjourned."

Jessy heard someone mutter, "The mayor is right. We don't want this town turning black."

People began to file out. Jessy sat wrapped in a feeling of actual pain for Joe. As he walked by her, his eyes were downcast.

Lilli stood up. Her voice was icy. "Lombard Hale is a rat."

Like a robot, Jessy got to her own feet. Outside, she and Lilli walked several blocks in silence. Finally, Lilli said, her voice still chill, "Dictator Hale had his way again. *Town* meeting my foot. It is Hale's show all the way. Whatever he wants, he gets. But you know, Jessy, poor Joe's case was settled before tonight."

"What do you mean, Lilli?" It was an automatic response.

"There's something new in town," Lilli told her, "a so-called businessmen's club. A minister from Oklahoma moved into the hotel a while back, *not* my place. He's gotten together with Lombard Hale almost every day since. Sometimes Hale takes Cecil Kinglake with him, sometimes Mr. Pierce and others. Rumor has it that they've formed the 'Ardensville Businessmen's Association.' A very private little clatch. About an hour before tonight's meeting they arranged to buy the livery as a co-op. A cooperative, all of them running it. And that's only part of their activities—"

"You mean—Joe was out of it—he didn't have a chance?"

Lilli shook her head, "Not with the Klan against him."

Jessy halted. "Darn it, Lilli, there you go again! I thought you said Hale and this minister had formed a businessmen's association?"

"Sorry I confused you, kid. The Klan often gets *started* this way. A Klan organizer from outside comes into a community to find out what's worrying its leaders. He offers the Ku Klux Klan as a way of solving things. But it's a secret club, so what people see is The Trade Association of Johnstown or The Sunshine Club of Burack City."

At the telephone office, Jessy reached for the doorknob and turned to face Lilli. "You won't misunderstand me, will you?"

Lilli tilted her head, waiting. Jessy struggled for the right words. "Granted, you read a lot, you're smart, Lilli. You're a writer with an awfully big imagination. Too big, it seems to me. Ardensville may have problems, but as far as anything like the Ku Klux Klan being here, I just don't believe that. I don't."

She drew a breath and added, "In the old days, the Klan tarred and feathered people, beat them, hung them. That's not happening here. It's just Hale, like you say, running the town his way."

Lilli unexpectedly caught her hand. "All right, child, if that's what you want to think. I am a writer"—she said it proudly—"I admit I have a vivid imagination. On the other hand, people come and go at my boarding house. I overhear things. I see things. And I can add two and two. Sometimes even four and four."

"I'm sorry, Lilli," Jessy said quickly. "I didn't mean to—It's just that I don't *want* you to be right."

"If I am wrong"—Lilli didn't smile—"I'll eat my new fur muff, with jelly on it."

Later that night, Cowboy played on the floor of the lamplit bathroom with a yarn ball Jessy had made for him, while she ran the tub full and hot. Letting her clothes drop to the floor, she climbed into the tub. For a long while she lay back, trying to keep her mind a blank as the hot water melted the tightness in her muscles.

A vision of home, The Ranch, began to fill Jessy's mind then. Without half trying, she could picture, feel, Mama's warm safe kitchen, hear the family chatter, smell the good cooking. It would be nice to go home to The Ranch for Christmas. She'd ask Gussie tomorrow if she could have the time off. It might even be—different for her there, now. If it was—she could stay there. She wouldn't have to come back here, to this Klan fuss.

"I can't, Jessamyn, I really can't let you go now," Mrs. Stuberg told Jessy when she asked. "An' I know how much family means this time of year, too. The board'll be extra busy, you see, with everybody and their brother callin' folks to wish 'em Merry Christmas an' all." She shook her head. "This ain't no time to be thinking about going someplace, weatherwise, anyhow. These little snow showers Ma Nature's been stirring up lately is just a warnin' that she's got bigger stuff for us, any day."

No matter what she tried to do—it didn't work out.

Jessy did her best to swallow her disappointment at not going home. From Mandy's radio that noon, a tinny-voiced man announced the snowstorm Gussie had predicted.

In a few days, it was blizzarding in earnest, the snow piled up outside, and Jessy found herself busier than ever at the switchboard. She made general announcements of meeting cancellations, one of them for the Ardensville Businessmen's Association. If this group actually was the Ku Klux Klan, Jessy realized, their activities were at a standstill for as long as the storm lasted.

Gussie dug up an extra headset and stool and joined Jessamyn at the switchboard. "It's only a matter of time," she warned, "before the heavy snow brings lines down. Service is going to be spotty, and if this storm don't let up we may not be givin' any at all. Better help folks while we can."

Following the radio announcer's advice, Jessy warned those wanting to travel to stay home. To families already snowed in and unable to get out, she arranged to send aid parties with fuel and food. At this worst of all times, it seemed to her, there was a maddening number of illnesses. Taking the calls as the hours of the storm wore on, routing the doctor to the people who needed him most, was like putting together the pieces of a demanding puzzle.

Mealtimes, Jessy bundled up and trudged through the snow to Mandy's for sandwiches and hot coffee for herself and Mrs. Stuberg, and they ate at the board.

Biting tiredly into a roast beef sandwich the fourth day of the storm, Jessy saw Gussie stiffen beside her. "Yes, Mrs. Pierce," Mrs. Stuberg said in a loud voice, "I understand. Now you calm down. Hear? Sure we will." She nodded. "Right away as soon as we hear something. We will let you know. Don't worry, Mrs. Pierce, it may not be so bad as all that." Mrs. Stuberg withdrew the plug. She shook her head. "Woman's gone all to pieces," she told Jessy.

Jessy quickly completed the call she was taking and asked, "What's wrong? What's happened at the Pierces'?"

"Wilford Pierce has been in Denver on business. He ought've stayed there, but he tried to come home. His train's vanished, must be stalled in heavy snowdrifts out west between here and Denver. Miz Pierce just heard it over the radio. She's worried sick about her man. She wants us to let her know right off if we hear anything about the train through our board."

Jessy wondered what would happen if Mr. Pierce left the train to try to reach a farm, a telephone, to find help. In a blizzard you could die going just a short way. And if he stayed with the train was there a stove, fuel enough? What about the others on the train? It was stranded out on the plains north and west, between Ardensville and Denver. How far out on the plains? "Mrs.

Stuberg, just where is the train stalled? Did Mrs. Pierce have any idea?"

"Radio says maybe ten, fifteen miles west. Not far the other side of the border, they think, in Colorado."

"Good! Bar M, Bar M," she mumbled to herself, ignoring Gussie's startled look. "I hope to heaven that line isn't down."

"Three longs and a short," Gussie said dryly, but Jessamyn was already making the connection, pushing the key.

"The line isn't dead," Jessy told her boss. In another minute she added, "But nobody's taking the phone down to answer." *Please, please*, she begged silently, and rang four more times. Suddenly, the faraway jangle was halted by a strong male voice, "H'lo? Bar M. A-a the boss ain't home. Mr. Moorehouse and his wife Etta are at their daughter's in Topeka. This is their foreman, Hatcher Elroy, speakin'."

Chapter 11

EVEN IN A MOMENT of crisis, Jessy felt a warm stirring inside at the sound of the cowboy's voice. "H-Hatch?" she said, "Mr. Elroy? This is the Ardensville telephone operator, Jessamyn Faber. You might not remember me, but—"

"I remember you."

"Oh. I—I—" She got herself in hand. "I called to tell you that there's a train stalled out your way, stuck in bad drifts. A train from Denver, headed for Ardensville. I have an idea it may not be far from the Bar M. You must know where the tracks lay, anyway. Could you get some men together, take some of your cowboys, and go find the train? Those passengers are stranded, probably freezing, and hungry. It may be a while before others get to them."

"We'll dig them out, don't worry," Hatch said. "I'm on my way, Miss. Good-bye."

Jessy tried to thank him, but Hatch Elroy was already off the line.

A knock on the telephone office door while she was on duty, two days later, made Jessy look up. Hatch Elroy stood there on the other side of the glass, grinning, heavily bundled and covered with snowflakes from his stetson down to his boots. For a second it seemed like a dream. Then Jessy recovered and with a hesitant motion of her hand signaled for him to come in.

"I wanted to tell you myself all of them folks on that train is all right," he said, closing the door quickly against the cold. But even the brief blast of frigid air was too much for the kitten, Cowboy. The little gray cat scampered for Jessy's bedroom, in back.

"Th-thank you. When I heard about the train, I—I thought of you right away."

"I hear there's a case or two of pneumonia and some with sniffles, but nobody froze. Thanks to you, we got there in time."

Jessy nodded. She had to turn away from him to take care of a call. He said to her back, "The boss' wife, Etta, couldn't get to town with the car or the buggy, so she sent me in on my horse. I'm supposed to pick up some things for her, like for Christmas—sewing folderol and cooking supplies. I could use a lady's know-how, if you all could come with me?"

Jessy stared unseeing at the board, the cords, in front of her. "I can't," she said in a small voice, "I can't leave the switchboard." She turned very fast to look at him. "Until noon," she thought to say quickly.

"Oh," he drawled, "that's fine. I got some other things to tend to till then. I'll come back for you."

What was so hard, Jessy wondered later, with a small inward smile, about buying a few yards of white broadcloth, lace, red thread, and some sugar and cooking chocolate? It was fun helping Hatch, all the same. He insisted on taking her to Mandy's for lunch, to repay her, and after a slight hesitation, Jessy consented.

Her midday meal hour was over much too soon. And yet, when Hatch fumblingly asked if he might see her again, it was as though a clamp suddenly came over her happy feelings. "I'm sorry," she said, with a shake of her head. It was one thing to think about the cowboy all the time, quite another to let him come courting her. She couldn't, wouldn't, go through that again.

"You ain't married, are you? Or promised?" he asked.

She shook her head. "It isn't that, or you. I—I'm trying to— I'm getting over something. It's best if I don't go out with anyone."

He looked perplexed. But he said quietly, "You're the boss."

Within an hour after her return to work, Jessy hated herself. Why did she turn him down? Why? She could have let him come calling. What would it hurt? He was all she could think about anymore, anyway. Was that any different? She'd like to see him, except now she'd probably never get another chance. He looked like the kind who would take her at her word. To him, "no" would mean that, "no." Forever.

She cried herself to sleep that night, for a brand new reason.

IT SEEMED TO JESSY that the entire town was in the Ardensville Public School Auditorium for the annual Christmas pageant. She'd come at Gussie's urging; the extra night off was a Christmas present from her boss. Lilli had said she would meet her with a "surprise."

Jessy searched the crowd as she headed down the aisle. Joe Cooke was seated near the back. He nodded at her, and Jessy smiled. Finally, several rows toward the front, Jessy spotted a familiar blonde head with a coronet of braids sparked with a small green bow. Lilli turned and saw her in the same moment. She motioned Jessy to take the seat beside herself and a handsome gentleman Jessy had never seen before.

Lilli leaned eagerly forward the moment Jessy was seated. "I'd like you to meet my friend, Bill Washburn. Mr. Washburn is a traveling salesman. He's taking a room at my board house until after the holidays. Bill—my good friend, Jessamyn."

Bill Washburn's gray suit complimented his graying brown hair and soft brown eyes. He winked at Jessy. "Nice to meet you," he told her, his voice warm with friendliness. He was quite a bit older than Lilli, Jessy thought, but it was easy to see why Lilli liked him. He was the sort of person you felt at ease with from the start. She felt a stab of envy, and remorse, that she wasn't sitting here with Hatcher Elroy.

On stage, a large chorus of children began to sing "Silent Night." Jessy settled back, knowing she would enjoy herself. She liked to see amateur plays and programs. For one thing, she'd always admired anyone who could perform before a crowd. She had never found that easy, herself. Yet, as part of the audience, she identified directly with players on stage. Her whole being suffered missed cues and awkward movements. When a flash of special talent showed on stage, it touched her, brought her close to tears of shared triumph. Tonight, the children's voices were especially beautiful.

She picked out Joe's two sons, Edwin and Harry, in a large group of singing angels dressed in gauzy blue with stiff gold wings. After a moment, the chorus swung into a peppy rendition of "Good King Wenceslas," and she now spotted Christopher, Althea, and little Delphine. She hadn't been able to visit the Salonikas for a long time. The bad snow had kept her busy at the telephone office.

A quick search of the audience, and she saw Lucian leaning against the wall in back. He looked well, and happy. Joe sat not far from him, pride showed in the way he sat, shoulders high, chin lifted, as though, too, he didn't want to miss a single note of the sweetly singing voices.

With embarrassment and shame, Jessy remembered Joe's treatment at the town meeting. He was probably too good for this town, if the truth were known. He ought to go somewhere else. But maybe her solution for troubles, to go away from them wasn't for everybody. Jessy turned her attention back to the stage, and she let herself get carried away in the old story of Jesus' birth.

At the end of the scene, there was a sudden gasp from the back of the room and a rustling noise that made Jessy turn to look. A half-dozen men in white sheets, holes cut for their eyes, swept up the center aisle. For a second, Jessy thought they were a part of the program. Beside her, Lilli gasped sharply, "Oh, no!"

The Klan! Jessy reached for Lilli's arm and held on. The sheeted men tromped to the stage and onto it while children stood frozen and wide-eyed like painted wooden toys, Jessy looked for someone in the audience to object. Nobody moved.

A large man in a sheet came to center stage, his fist raised. "What are you thinking of, you mothers and fathers out there?" he stormed. Was it Hale? It sounded like him, Jessy thought. In a voice thick with outrage, the man continued, "Spawn of foreign blood. Black-skinned pickaninnies! Taking part in a program with your own sweet white babies. Are you blind, people? Or are you afraid to make them keep their place? If you are not able to stand up to the human garbage in our midst, we will do it for you."

"No!" Jessy tried to protest, but no sound would come out.

"Coward, hiding under a sheet," Lilli hissed.

"We are your protection, good people," the voice up front shouted. "Here to preserve your values, and long-standing traditions. We will not allow outsiders to weaken and destroy this lovely land."

"I want to do *something*," Lilli told Jessy with anguish, "but I'm afraid I'm going to be sick."

"I know." Jessy reached to squeeze her friend's hand and found it as cold as her own.

There was a sudden scuffling, shuffling on the stage. Sharp whispers carried out into the crowd. "Send these urchins home. Get them out of here." Jessy's vision blurred as the deepest shame she'd ever felt overwhelmed her.

When the men in white tromped out, back the way they'd come, to Jessy's amazement, thin, trembling voices began to sing again, under the direction of a scared-looking teacher. There were empty places where Edwin and Harry had stood. The Salonikas, too, had vanished. The singing children moved together to fill in the gaps.

For a few minutes Jessy was dazed. She jerked to her feet then, and turning, saw that Lucian was gone from the room; Joe Cooke, too. Some of the people in the audience looked like frightened statues, a few appeared not to care, and worse—some looked proud and thankful for what had taken place.

"Jessy, wait, we'll come with you," Lilli cried in a whisper, but Jessy pulled free and ran toward the door. The children were her friends. If this wasn't their place, it wasn't for her either.

In the telephone office, she scooped Cowboy into her arms and rushed by Gussie at the switchboard, murmuring only that she was all right and to please leave her alone. Shut in her room, Jessy hugged the kitten and rocked back and forth on the cot. "It—it was the ugliest thing—why did we all just sit there? I care, Cowboy," she whispered brokenly to the fuzzy, wriggling kitten. "I care so much. But I can't think, can't do anything I should—"

She felt like a tired zombie next day, Christmas day, but the switchboard was jammed with calls and she was too busy to think—to worry about the Ku Klux Klan, to miss her family, to feel torn with feeling about Hatch, about anything.

Lilli came a few days later and begged Jessy to move into the boarding house. But Jessy insisted she was snug and comfy where she was. "I've gotten used to this cramped little box," she told her friend. It's home to me now." They did not talk about the Ku Klux Klan. It was only too obvious that the Invisible Empire was very much present in Ardensville.

As soon as the flood of holiday work slowed, Jessy visited the snowy church woods. She was surprised and pleased to find the coal shed transformed into a reasonably snug brick cottage. Under Lucian's direction, the children had used old bricks from the tumbledown church to build a tight, outside wall about the shed.

The little girls pointed with pride to a second metal drum that Lucian had made into a heating stove; the first they'd had before, for cooking. They were all right, from the weather. The Ku Klux Klan was another matter.

She hated even thinking of the pageant, but she made herself ask, "Has anyone, those men—in white sheets, done anything? Have they bothered you since Christmas?" It was hard to meet Lucian's eyes.

"No," he told her slowly, his face going red, his eyes angry. "They got done what they were there for, that night. It may not be the end of it, but I don't care. They'll find that trying to run us out of town won't work."

Jessy twisted uneasily in her chair. "Lucian, those men aren't silly, wishy-washy weaklings. In the past the Ku Klux Klan has been known to—do terrible things. They could again. As a group they—listen, Luc, maybe you should—"

"No." Lucian had the look of a ferocious young pup. "We won't leave, if that's what you're about to say, Jessamyn."

She sat back, thoughtful for several minutes. "If you won't do that, Lucian, do you have other family to look out for you? Someone older, a grownup? You do have to think of the little kids. I know your parents are—gone. But I've been thinking—you must have other relatives?"

"A whole flock of them in Greece," Lucian told her with a wry smile. "A bit too far from here, isn't it? Grandma Salonika is still there."

"None in this country? None at all?"

He seemed reluctant to tell her. "We have an Uncle Julio living in New York. But that's still a long way from Kansas."

New York was not so far from Kansas by telephone, Jessy was thinking as she returned to work. Julio Salonika! Would the uncle come here, if she asked? The Salonikas needed care, with-them-all-the-time care. For that, a blood relative was best. She could take care of this!

The next time she visited the church woods, Jessy casually asked Lucian, "Is your Uncle Julio, the one in New York, married?" An aunt to mother these children would be perfect. Lucian looked at her strangely for a full minute. Jessy worried that he guessed what she was up to. She gave him an innocent smile.

"No aunt," he told her. "Uncle Julio is a bachelor." He added with a knowing grin, "But he's too old and not right for you, Jessamyn."

So that's what he thought. Jessy turned pink; at the same time feeling let down that Julio Salonika was a bachelor. A kind, elderly man without a wife, though, would be better than no family at all.

In two more visits, making idle conversation with first one Salonika, then another, Jessy had enough information about Julio Salonika's whereabouts in New York to try and reach him. The rest would have to be up to Julio, himself.

Chapter 12

EARLY ONE MORNING, before her work day at the switch-board had begun, Jessy took the plunge and made the call, East. Ignoring the squeaks and squawks, the fade in, fade out of the weak connection, she talked nearly fifteen minutes. To her vast relief, the faraway male voice agreed. He would come. And yes, if she wanted, he would keep it a secret that she had asked for his help.

The elder Salonika arrived by train in Ardensville in Febru-ary. The same day, an hour or two after the train came in, Althea and Delphine appeared at the telephone office door. When she let them in, Jessy could see that the little girls were electrified with excitement. "Uncle Julio came!" Althea cried. "He said he'd been planning to come for the longest time, and now—he's here! We want you to meet him, Jessy-Central. On your next day off."

"I'd love t—" Jessy tried to answer, but Delphine was giggling and jumping up and down.

"Althea and me are going to have a party! For our Uncle Julio. He's a nice man, Jess'yn. And fun. Uncle Julio, he said"—she threw out her chest and made her voice deep—"'Yes, we got to do something special. I want to meet your best friend, Jess'yn, the Central.'"

Jessy laughed. "I've been wanting to meet your Uncle, too. I'm so glad he's with you, to look out for—well, anyway, I would love to come to your party. I'd like to bring something. Any suggestions?"

Althea shook her head. "Nothing, Jessy, please. I know what 'freshments we'll fix. We're going to make our house pretty, too. You just come." Looking worried that she might have hurt Jessy's feelings, Althea added, "All right?"

"Of course it's all right. I know you're a good fixer, Althea. And I am looking forward to your party!" She gave a weary stage sigh. "The rest of the week will go slow for me, I just know." She winked. "But I'll be there, with bells on."

When Jessy arrived, the woods, usually as quiet as a funeral parlor, was noisy with music. Feeling uncertain, yet curious, she zigzagged along the path to the cottage. The little building seemed to swell from a joyful mix of fast piano, banjo, and horns. Whatever could be going on?

Jessy knocked three times before they heard her. Althea let her in. "We're helping Uncle Julio unpack," Delphine said, flying around the noisy, cluttered room like an excited bird. "The train brought the rest of his pretty things, today. Lookit, Jessy!"

Jessy could not look away from Uncle Julio. The only man in the room, he was hardly thirty, not middle-aged. With black hair and olive skin, he was so handsome Jessy couldn't look into his eyes for fear of having her own read too clearly. What a surprise—

Julio Salonika was across the floor and taking her hand in an instant. "What a lovely sweet you are, Miss Faber," he said with a dazzling smile. "My nephews and nieces have been telling me what a kind person, what a pretty girl you are. But not one word, glowing as they were, did you justice." To Jessamyn's dismay and embarrassment, he lifted her fingertips to his lips.

The children laughed as though hand kissing was the funniest thing they'd ever seen. In a corner, Chris stood by a piece of furniture almost as tall as he, with a flower-shaped horn on top. A gramophone! The boy began to crank a handle at the side, and a record began to play. "Go ahead and dance with her, Uncle Julio. Dance with Jessy!"

Her face grew hot. Jessy backed away from Uncle Julio, who bowed low before her. She shook her head. He must be crazy, to ship a Victrola all the way from New York to Kansas. This wasn't turning out the way she'd planned, at all. A grinning Lucian motioned for his little sisters to clear the middle of the small floor as Julio took Jessy into his arms.

The record blared forth the happiest, jiggliest melody Jessy had ever heard. Had she been dancing all her life? In a few minutes it felt that way. She took a deep breath. Around and around the room they bounced, bumped, and hopped. The children laughed and clapped. When young Chris' arm grew tired of cranking the Victrola, Lucian took his place.

"You, too, you, too," Uncle Julio good-naturedly ordered Chris, Althea, and Delphine onto the floor. "Watch now, watch us. Do what we're doing. Right. That's it."

Exhilarated, breathless, Jessy tried later to escape to a chair as Lucian changed the record. A slow, wailing melody filled the room, reminding Jessy of the empty sad feeling she got listening to the lonely whistle of a freight train. "Blues," Julio said, sweeping Jessy into his arms once more.

When everyone except Uncle Julio was too tired to dance another step, Althea and Delphine brought their shaky table back to the middle of the room and served refreshments. On snowflake doilies the girls had cut from newspaper, they placed sugar-dusted pancakes rolled with applesauce inside. Over the rim of her coffee cup, Jessamyn told them, "Delicious, truly."

Her words brought a glow of satisfaction to Althea's face, and Delphine giggled.

Before going home, Jessy noted Julio Salonika's belongings piled about the walls. There was the Victrola and stacks of records. Three pair of very shiny shoes, one turned over so she could see a metal plate fastened to the bottom—dancing shoes! There were expensive-looking shirts and suits draped everywhere. Not in the least did Julio resemble the man she had hoped she was bringing here. Jessy sighed. What had she done?

It was wrong to jump to conclusions, though. In a while she'd know better, if she had done the right thing.

Jessamyn visited the Salonikas whenever she could in the days that followed, wanting to see for herself if the arrangement was working out. Also, she must admit, she felt drawn there by Julio Salonika. Dashing, devil-may-care, he was the funniest, most likable person she had ever met. Anyone would be fascinated by the man's stories of his travels and escapades.

Before long, however, she could see that her earlier fears were well-grounded. Plainly, Julio was a handsome, charming ne'r-do-well, who was not going to be much help to the younger Salonikas. A dance instructor by trade, it was not his fault, he insisted one evening, that "hick-town Ardensville" felt no need for a dance studio. He couldn't work at anything else.

Jessy began to wish she'd left well enough alone. Then one wintry day, she ran into Lucian coming from the post office. He wore a radiant smile. Had Julio gone? "What happened? You look like the cat that got all the cream, Luc."

He looked too overcome with joy to speak, but words finally tumbled out, "G-good news!" He waved the letter he held. "Good news."

"Well, what?" She laughed. "What's your good news about?"

Lucian couldn't stop grinning. "This is from Grandma Salonika," he told Jessy. "She—she is coming to live with us. On the train next week. She is coming, for good. I wrote to her when—when Mama and Papa died. It has taken her more than two y-years." He drew a long breath. "But Grandmother has saved the m-money. She's on the way."

"Oh, Lucian, that's wonderful! If I had known you had written for your grandmother to come...." Jessy hesitated.

He looked into her eyes. "I know you sent for Uncle Julio, I guessed right away. If you hadn't kept it a secret that you were sending for him, I could have told you how it would be."

"I'm sorry. I wish I hadn't been in such a hurry, but—"

"Don't worry. Everything will be better now that Grandma is coming. I got to let the kids know." He started off, his short wiry frame swinging.

Jessy watched him go, feeling a glow of pleasure herself. "I want to meet your grandmother when she gets here," she shouted after him.

Lucian turned and bounced backward a few steps. "Come with us to the depot to meet her train. Next week, Thursday. The noon train." He waved.

Some things were looking better, anyway, Jessy thought, sighing. She waved back.

A SOFT CLEAN SMELL of melting snow filled the air that next Thursday as Jessy waited at the depot with the Salonika children and their Uncle Julio. They'd been told by the station master that the train from the East would be almost an hour late. She had gone back to the telephone office to ask Gussie to work an extra hour or so for her, then Jessy returned to the depot.

Julio Salonika fidgeted. "Mrs. Beecroft wanted me to have lunch with her today. If I had known the train would be late— Oh, I ought to've stayed at her house. I let Mrs. Beecroft down."

"Worse if you let Grandma down by not being here, Uncle," Lucian said calmly. "Mrs. Beecroft will get over it. Anyway, one lady friend less won't make a difference For the short time you've been here, you've done all right. Every available lady in town has invited you to dinner at least once."

"You exaggerate," Julio said with a frown. "Listen, I think the blasted train is finally coming."

Jessy, too, could hear the far-off rumble, and seconds later, a keening whistle. She smiled as the smaller children laughed and poked at one another. Lucian waited with a glad, quiet grin. The train ground to a chuffing halt on the tracks before them moments later. The younger children quieted suddenly and watched wide-eyed as passengers began to alight.

A drummer in a rumpled suit, carrying a case in each hand, no doubt sample merchandise to show at local stores, came first. A rosy-cheeked, plump, pretty young woman stepped down. She was rewarded with an especially appreciative glance from Uncle Julio, in spite of the fact that two children clung to her skirts and another slept in her arms. An elderly man came next, poking a white cane before him. A pair of prosperous-looking ranchers in gray stetsons followed the blind man.

"She ain't come," Delphine said in a stricken whisper. "Grandmother ain't come."

"Where is she?" Althea asked Lucian plaintively.

He started to speak, but something he saw stopped him. "There—is—our grandma, I think."

She was a short, elderly woman—Jessy saw her now, too. Under the burden of a heavy coat and two basketweave valises, she swayed off the train. Tufts of silvery hair showed beneath the kerchief knotted at the back of her head. There was fear in the small wrinkled face. Jessy started forward. "Mrs. Salonika?"

Julio, exchanging pleasantries with the comely housewife, shook off Jessy's hand as she tried to pull him along. "Your mother," Jessy said, and he came. Lucian, the younger ones in tow, ran.

Suddenly seeing them, the old woman let out a sharp cry and dropped her bags. Laughing, half-sobbing, calling to them in her native tongue, the woman trotted forward and tried to gather all of the children into her arms. Jessy recognized the word, "Julio!" when Mrs. Salonika spotted him over Chris' shoulder. Releasing the youngsters, she bustled to her son and held him close. It must have been many years since Julio had seen his mother, Jessy thought. He acted as if he would be more comfortable in the young housewife's arms.

The little group parted, and Lucian brought his grandmother to Jessy. The boy spoke in Greek to his grandmother and touched Jessy's arm at the same time. Grandma Salonika smiled and murmured a soft word Jessy didn't know. But it was a greeting, a nice greeting. "I'm glad to know her," Jessy responded. "Tell her she is welcome here, we are so glad she's come." On impulse, Jessy caught the woman's small withered hand and clasped it warmly. Seeing the Salonika children's faces, Jessy knew with glad certainty that Grandma's coming was a very good thing.

Julio busily divided his mother's things amongst his nieces and nephews to carry, leaving himself free. Jessy shook her head. In that instant she heard a familiar voice to her right. It was Lombard Hale, meeting the ranchers. Spotting her, he smiled and tipped his hat. Then his glance traveled from Jessy to the Salonika children, to their uncle and grandmother. He visibly stiffened, and the smile left his face.

A tremor raced down Jessy's spine when Hale interrupted his rancher friends' conversation, remarking loudly, "Something is causing a flood of foreigners—"

The Salonikas were too busy chattering to hear. The ranchers, nodding indifferently, went back to their conversation.

Jessy put an arm through Lucian's and caught Grandma Salonika's elbow in her other hand. "Let's go to Mandy's," she said, her heart pounding. "My treat." She urged the younger ones to come along fast with a motion of her head. "You can order anything you like, all right?" Grandma's soft brown eyes, turned on Jessy, looked puzzled.

Lucian interpreted in halting Greek. "*Kafeneion*, Grandmother. Coffee shop. We have some *coffee*, get warm and rest before we go home."

A look of delight filled the old woman's face. "*Kafe*," she said with an affirmative nod. "We—get—*kafe*."

"Mandy," Julio grumbled, bringing up the rear, "does not fix one thing I am able to eat. The girl is pert in her own way, though." Julio seemed to be talking to himself. "No husband. If Mandy could cook dishes not so—so common." Jessy smiled back at him, but Julio was too buried in romantic thoughts to notice.

Jessy felt uneasy at Mandy's. She hadn't stopped to think how Julio's and Grandmother Salonika's coming to Ardensville would affect the mayor. Of course he wouldn't like it. Jessy was glad when everyone finished the raisin pie and coffee. She didn't know what she would do if Hale should come into the restaurant. She wished she had the courage to stand up and tell him a few things. But after that other time, she might not ever have the nerve again.

Outside on the sidewalk, the Salonikas urged Jessamyn to come along home with them. She gently refused. "This is for you, for family," she told Lucian, Christopher, and the little girls. "You have catching up to do with your grandmother. And she has traveled a long way. I'm sure she'll welcome a chance to rest. I'll come another time."

In the next weeks, the long winter began to break up, the cold easing. Going about town, Jessy was sure she could smell spring close at hand. She could hardly wait. One noon she sat alone at a window table in Mandy's, feeling lazy and thoughtful.

Grandmother Salonika was a fine person. She heaped good food and love on her grandchildren and already they had taken on a look Jessy couldn't quite name. A healthy, happy wholeness she decided. Plans were afoot to frame up a large, two-room addition to the coal shed. Of course, Julio wanted no part of it. He spent longer and longer periods away at a lady friend's so he wouldn't have to help.

Jessy stared out the window, sipped her tea, and remembered a warm day late last summer. She'd had a picnic by herself in the country, she'd gone wading, and…. Suddenly, Jessy could see again Hatcher Elroy's blue eyes watching her, feel his hand on her foot as he tried to take out the bloodsucker. Even now she could feel his closeness. Jessy put her cup down, and it rattled in the saucer.

Why had she told him he couldn't see her?

A flurry of white outside on the street brought Jessy's reverie to an abrupt end. A man in a sheet. *No.* Another, more, they were everywhere! She choked back a small cry, then watched, frozen.

Chapter 13

A HORSE-DRAWN WAGON drew up. A sheeted specter climbed onto the wagon seat. With raised fists he began his speech. Others, not the Klan, hurried to hear. Jessy clutched the table edge, as hard words and phrases came into the cafe: "Enemies from abroad to take our jobs, our land." And, "Immoral—clean up *now*. Break heads if necessary for justice!"

Other diners shambled out of the cafe to listen. Mandy stood for a moment, looking out, then she returned to the kitchen with a grunt of disgust.

Jessy stayed where she was. Suddenly, her view was blocked by a wraithlike figure that halted just outside the window. Anna Cora Hale. Her arms were wrapped tight about her body. Jessy tapped on the window. It startled Anna Cora, but when she whirled and saw Jessy, she looked relieved. Jessy motioned for her to come into the cafe. It wouldn't be as scary as out there.

Anna Cora tumbled in, looked uncertain, then she hurtled toward Jessy's table like a child seeking the safety of a mother's arms. "Here," Jessy said, "sit close by me."

Anna Cora bumped her chair close against Jessy's and sat down, trembling. Jessy took Anna Cora's hands, so cold, into her own. She could think of nothing to say. Among the sheeted crowd outside was Anna Cora's father, with little doubt. And probably Cecil Kinglake as well. Minutes ago, she had recognized the handyman's walk. Even under a sheet, Cecil couldn't hide. Did Anna know?

In a shaky voice, Anna broke the silence. "I—I don't think they should do that out there. They—they are sc-scaring people. Those m-men look like ghosts. They shouldn't do that. Yelling. Saying bad things to scare people."

Jessy nodded. It was a puzzle to her, why people couldn't live side by side, peaceably. Shouldn't justice be an attempt to get along, not a call for blood like out there?

The demonstration seemed to last a lifetime, but it was over within the hour. A deathlike quiet settled over the street as it emptied. "They're gone." Anna Cora whispered, "all gone." Her eyes clouded. "I wonder if father saw it. I'm going to tell Daddy."

Jessy put an arm across Anna Cora's shoulder and squeezed, wordless. Let Lombard Hale explain this to his daughter, if he could. Jessy stood up, feeling old and tired. She drew Anna Cora to her feet at the same time. She was startled, but managed a soft smile, when Anna Cora jerked about to catch her body in a fierce, childlike hug. "Thank you for helping me feel not so scared, Central. I'm going home."

"'Bye, Anna."

That night a cross was burned on a knoll west of town. Toward dawn several homes were pelted with stones, the families within warned to leave town. Without being told, Jessy knew who the families were: the Salonikas, Joe and his boys, Isaac Burmann, the Irish Catholic McGuire family, a few others. Luckily, no one was hurt.

When none of the families, and at the switchboard Jessy was in a position to know, heeded the Klan's threats to leave town, some of the fearfulness inside Jessy let go.

One afternoon, Lucian stopped by the telephone office to tell Jessamyn his grandmother would like her to take supper with them the next night. Jessy accepted gladly. Worry about the Ku Klux Klan for a week now had been closing her in. She decided to make the most of her evening out. Uncle Julio, self-centered though he was, could make things lively and fun. She hoped he'd want to dance. She might even buy a new, ready-made dress, Jessy decided.

Except for the small bearded owner and herself, Burmann's Department Store was empty of human souls when she entered that same evening. Odd, Jessy thought. This time of year house-wives were usually buying yards of dimity and gingham—ribbons and buttons for new outfits. Fashionable spring hats. "Where is everybody, tonight, Mr. Burmann?" Jessy asked loudly, for the merchant was hard of hearing.

"At Grant's Emporium, I am afraid," he told her. "Their sale on shoes, it is very good, I understand." The merchant smiled as if to show he didn't mind. But he couldn't hide the worry Jessy saw in his eyes.

"What's wrong?" she asked. "Are you sure—?"

Mr. Burmann stroked his beard. His hands shook as he reached out to straighten a stack of shirts on top of the display case. "The Klan spreads word that people must not buy from me," he told her. "I am Jew. So they boycott my store."

"Folks are doing what the Klan wants?"

"*Oy,*" he groaned. "Business has fallen to nothing almost. Why do they do this?" he implored, palms turned up. "I have been here ten years. A few loyal friends they buy from me. But it is not enough to support the store. Why all of a sudden everything have to change? Ardensville for a long time is my home!"

"I am sorry, Mr. Burmann." Saying she was sorry seemed—not enough. "Th-this thing has gotten so ugly," she added. "Something has to happen soon to—turn it around. I would think the—the government, the leaders in the state, *somebody* would do something about the Ku Klux Klan."

The merchant's expression turned hopeful. "Over at Emporia, William White is running for governor. I think people will pay attention to him. They say he is 'burning the Kluxer's nightie tails' with his speeches."

"Good! Mr. Burmann, don't let the Klan beat you down." She was practically shouting, only partly because Isaac was hard of hearing. "If you don't give in to them, when it's over, you'll still have your store!"

"Bravo! Jessy, is that really you?"

Jessy said, turning to see Lilli Miller, "I was just letting Mr. Burmann know how I feel."

"Didn't know you were a fighter."

Jessy shrugged. "Maybe I am a cream puff inside, but nobody likes to see good people bullied."

"Well said, kiddo. Mr. Burmann, you should do what Jessy says. From what I read, our governor is very much against the Klan, and a lot of good decent folks agree with him."

Jessy wanted to ask where these other good people were, but a smile filled Mr. Burmann's face. "You make my day better. Now, you come for what? I show you?"

"A new dress!" Jessy told him, relieved to change the subject. She looked toward the racks. "If you have something in yellow? With white trim, maybe. And belted, not a sash that ties. I saw one like that in here before."

"Unmentionables," Lilli told Mr. Burmann, straight-faced. She added brazenly, "Lots of lace, slinky, pink, the prettiest undies in your store." She burst out laughing at herself. "Come on, kiddo"—she grabbed Jessy's arm—"let's buy the store out. We'll make up for the scaredy-cats who won't come in here."

"Well, I do need the dress. And maybe some stockings. A ribbon—"

FEELING FESTIVE and pretty, Jessy wore her new yellow dress to supper at the Salonikas. "Something smells very good," Jessy said as Althea took her coat.

The little girl looked pleased. "Grandma is cooking special for you. A chicken and potato stew like she made for company in Greece. For dessert there is a—a pudding that Grandma calls *krema*. You'll like it, Jessamyn."

"I know I will." Jessy smiled at Grandmother Salonika who bustled about the tiny kitchen area of the room. The old woman hesitated just long enough to give Jessy a bright smile and flip her apron in a bit of a curtsy, then, humming softly, she went back to her cooking.

Jessy looked around. What a change! Red-checked curtains framed new windows Grandma Salonika had ordered set into the front wall, one on either side of the door. The room that used to be dingy from coal dust was spectacularly clean and filled with light. Colorful rag rugs dotted the well-scrubbed floor. A cut-glass bowl, empty of flowers, centered the lace-covered table, but light dancing on the glass of the bowl made its own bouquet.

Delphine and Althea took Jessy's hands to lead her to their one upholstered chair. Giggling, they sat on the arms. Giving each of them a hug, she said, "You are so lucky to have your Grandmother come live with you and take care of you. Tell me what you are up to these days? How is school?"

They babbled for several minutes about an upcoming spelling bee, then brought out paper dolls they were cutting from an old magazine. Delphine showed Jessy a small scab on her knee that she'd gotten in a fall.

"Where are your brothers, and your Uncle Julio?" Jessy asked after a while.

Delphine just looked at her; Althea frowned and shrugged.

"Where are they?" Jessy asked again.

Althea spoke quietly, "Lucian and Chris are gone to look for Uncle Julio again."

"Looking for Julio *again?* What do you mean, honey?"

"We have to set the table for Grandma now, Delphine," Althea said. She took her sister's hand and left Jessy sitting in puzzled silence. She would have to wait for Lucian.

Jessy was consoling Grandmother Salonika about her over-cooked meal when Lucian and Chris finally came, without Julio. Lucian spoke first to his grandmother, in Greek. She listened with an exasperated expression. Jessy couldn't understand what they were saying, but Grandmother Salonika, when Lucian was fin-ished, seemed satisfied. The little woman mumbled an exclama-tion, and with a motion of her hand indicated that they should forget the matter for the present.

After supper, Jessy drew Lucian aside. "What is this about your Uncle Julio? If you don't mind telling me, I'd like to know what's happened?"

"He's been gone several days," Lucian told her. "At first I was afraid something had happened to him" Silent for a moment, he scuffed his shoe back and forth, then went on, "I told the kids not to tell anybody he was missing until we found out something."

"When did he disappear, Luc?" Jessy asked, feeling cold. "Was it—was it the night of the Klan demonstration, when the cross was burned?"

Lucian looked at her for a long moment, then shook his head. "No. I thought about that, too, that the Ku Klux Klan might be part of it. I know well enough how they feel about—us. Uncle Julio came up missing after that. I've asked around. What I hear"—Lucian grinned shyly and his ears reddened—" makes me think it's something else. Julio was seeing a married lady with children. And others, lots of ladies. A mad husband might have ordered Uncle Julio to get out of town. And maybe Julio didn't have time enough to let us know he was leaving."

Jessy repressed a smile. "Julio might not be guilty of anything. From what I know about him, he is a—a very free spirit. An adventurer who likes to come and go as he pleases. He might've just taken off."

Lucian frowned. "That may be it. Uncle Julio is a bum, really. And not very thoughtful. It probably wouldn't enter his selfish head that he should let his family know what he's doing." Lucian was looking at his grandmother, concern and affection in his face.

Grandmother Salonika knows her son better than we do, Jessy was thinking. Aloud, she told Lucian, "If Julio really wants a dance studio, he'd be better off in a city larger than Ardensville. You'll get a letter from him soon, telling you that he is charming folks in some new town."

"You think so?" After a minute, Lucian smiled, and he didn't look as tense as earlier.

"In a way I envy your Uncle Julio. People like him have a wonderful life, happy-go-lucky wanderers. No worries."

A hint of resentment came to Lucian's eyes. "Well, we can't all be like that," he said. "Some of us have duties we can't run from."

She followed his glance to the others in the room. "Lucian to my mind, you're more of a man than Uncle Julio, even if he is older than you. You can be awfully proud of yourself. I'm proud of you. Your mother and father would be, too, the way you take care of Chris and the girls. It's a big job."

A while later, bidding them good-bye, Jessy said, "If I hear anything through the switchboard that will give us a more certain idea of where Julio's gone off to, I'll let you know. And then we can all stop worrying about him."

Jessy felt partly responsible. She was the one who had brought Julio Salonika to Ardensville. So she hoped the switchboard would spill a clue as to his whereabouts. It was common for sub-scribers to call in and let her know items of information they be-lieved would interest others. For several days Jessy listened with care and learned more than she wanted to know about symptoms of spring flu; the best methods to clean kitchen linoleum; and a must-see movie showing at the Orpheum, Douglas Fairbanks starring in *Robin Hood*.

Tidbits of gossip concerning domestic squabbles drifted in. With his reputation, Jessy was sure Julio could be involved in one of them, but he wasn't mentioned.

He'd simply gone off of his own free will, Jessy decided. And it might be years before his family knew where he had gone.

Chapter 14

OF LATE, JESSY REALIZED, she had been putting through an unusual number of calls from two local businessmen to out-of-town banks. Because of the Klan boycott, "undesirable merchants," as seen by the Ku Klux Klan, were having deep trouble. The businesses couldn't keep going without borrowed money to carry them.

With spring, there were more and more Ku Klux Klan parades and heated speeches promoting "head-breaking" to gain "one-hundred percent Americanism" and "jobs for Americans first." Lilli told her one day when they had gone together to Mandy's for a late evening snack that a lot of folks in Ardensville liked the fraternal aspects of the Klan and enjoyed the secretiveness of it. The idea of "rough stuff" excited them. People, Lilli insisted, were learning how to hate and show it as they never had before, and the Klan was the instructor.

Jessy pleaded, "Let's get away from all this, at least for a day. Please, Lilli. Let's go for a horseback ride in the country, or for a picnic. Let's go fishing. Anything."

"Sure, kid," Lilli was agreeable. "I plead guilty to neglecting our friendship lately." She toyed with her coffee. "You probably know that Bill Washburn has been in town again, for a long stay." With an innocent smile, she said, "I—I'm falling in love, I think." She returned Jessy's hug and went on, wistfully, "Bill had to go on another selling trip, though. He left yesterday, and I feel awful." She shrugged. "Whatever you want to do, I'm game."

"A picnic then. As far from town as we can get."

"Bill left me his roadster to drive while he's gone; he took the train back East. I've got a great idea!" Lilli exclaimed.

"What?"

"A down-home, amateur rodeo. I heard some ranchers who stayed at my place talking about it. It's contests—riding bucking horses, roping steers, racing and so on. Takes place almost every Sunday from early spring on, at a place called Oriel Creek Campground, where travelers camped in the old days. Sometimes a fiddler shows up and they dance; everybody brings a picnic dinner. Want to go? There'll be good-looking cowboys all over the place, every cowhand in the county goes—" She stopped suddenly, then went on, "Hey kid, from the look on your face I think I said a magic word. What was it—*cowboy?* Sure, Jess, if that's what you want. We'll go get you one."

"Shush," Jessy ordered with a laugh. "It's just that I'm happy we'll be getting out of town awhile. I am desperate. What time do we leave?" She'd never told Lilli about Hatch Elroy and wouldn't now. But if he should be there at Oriel Creek….

"*Early!*"

Jessy looked at Lilli, startled, as Lilli snapped her fingers close to her chin.

"I said 'early' three times and got no response," Lilli told her. "Where were you kid?"

Jessy had to think fast. "Wondering what to wear, what to fix for lunch; I was wishing Sunday was right now," she said in a fluster.

She decided to wear the new yellow dress. From Mr. Pierce's drugstore, she got shoe polish for her white pumps and coconut oil shampoo for her hair. She left her hair down for the special occasion and tied her cascade of coppery curls loosely with yellow ribbon.

The girls agreed that Jessy would bring roast beef sandwiches and angel food cake ordered from Mandy's, and Lilli would fix lemonade and potato salad, along with early fresh vegetables from her garden.

"Tell me about Bill Washburn," Jessy said when they were in his car, on their way. To enjoy the bright sunshine more, they drove with the windows down. "Do you think you'll marry him, Lilli?"

"I might if he asks me. Bill is kind," Lilli told her, "thoughtful, considerate—smarter than a lot of fellows."

"Are you writing any stories these days?" Jessy asked, thinking that Lilli might be exaggerating just a trifle about Bill.

"Always." Lilli looked away from the road at Jessy beside her. "I hope Bill won't mind, but I've put him in several stories. He's the perfect pattern for a dashing hero."

They drove in silence for a time, then Lilli said, "You'd never guess whose opinion I get. Who reads the stories before I send them to the true confession magazine. Make a guess, Jessy."

Looking out at the blue morning sky made Jessy think of Hatch Elroy's eyes. She asked absentmindedly, "Who, Lilli?"

"Gussie Stuberg."

Jessy almost choked. "When? Why?"

"The one and only Augusta Stuberg," Lilli said. "Since she was always haggling at me to spill some lurid details from my so-called 'past,' it seemed only natural she ought to read my stuff. No matter what I say, though, she still believes every word I write is true and about *me*. Can you believe it?"

"Lilli, you like putting on the scandalous flapper act and you know it," Jessy scolded affectionately. "Does Mrs. Stuberg like your stories, then?"

"Oh, yes!" Lilli's eyes danced. "And you know, Gussie makes some good suggestions. With the romantic parts, too. Since she and old Mr. Munker have been keeping company, she's becoming an expert. Or, maybe she's always been. She doesn't fit the picture, exactly, but Jessy, inside Gussie Stuberg there's a real belle!"

A while later they left the main highway and began to follow a long dusty road. New spring grass waved in a gentle wind; cattle dotted the flatness of the land. Windmills turned at watering tanks. "I love it," Jessy said softly, looking out. "I love ranch country. Do you, Lilli? At all?"

"Sorry. I favor the city. Ardensville is about as country as I can stand. But you, Jessy, you belong in country like this. You grew up on a ranch, didn't you tell me once?"

"Rented farms, mostly. But our own place that we have now, we call *The Ranch*." Jessy sighed, thoughtful. "I doubt The Ranch will ever be home to me again, though. When I left"—she bit her lip and tried again—"it seems I should find my own special place to settle now."

"Will it be Ardensville, for good?"

"Not the way things are," Jessy said with an emphatic shake of her head. "I'd like to stay. It's a pretty town, and I've come to like a lot of the people. But there's too much I don't like."

"The Ku Klux Klan?"

"Exactly."

"It's a terrible mess, all right," Lilli said soberly. "Somebody is going to get hurt bad, or killed, I'm afraid—" She broke off. "But let's not talk about them today."

Jessy smiled her thanks. "Shouldn't we be getting there?" she asked in another few minutes. "I feel like a little kid going to the circus."

From time to time, Jessy could feel Lilli's eyes on her, studying her. "Is it just the rodeo?" Lilli asked finally. "I don't think so," she answered herself. "You act like—Jessy, do you know somebody in particular you expect to be there?" She covered her mouth with her hand. "A cowboy!" she declared. "Don't deny it, Jessy, it's written all over your face!"

"Calm down, Lilli," Jessy chided softly. She couldn't help laughing. "I do know *of* a cowboy who might be at the rodeo. I ran into him a few times. That's all there is to it."

"Oh, no. Oh, no, that's not all there is to it," Lilli yelped. "You're the kind who ought to marry and settle down in ranch country someday, so you should be looking at cowboys and ranchers with—serious intent."

"Good grief, Lilli, slow down," Jessy protested. "No one said anything about getting married."

Lilli twirled a white-blonde wisp of hair around her finger and slid down a bit in the car seat. "And I was planning to be a bridesmaid," she mumbled.

Jessy doubled over, laughing. In a minute or two, Lilli jiggled her arm. "Look. I think that's the place. Up ahead, there." Lilli shaded her eyes and leaned toward the windshield. "I see a grove of trees. A couple cars—and—buggies and wagons. That's got to be it."

As they drew closer, Jessy could see for herself that the grounds were alive with people on foot and on horseback; others were clambering from farm wagons. In another minute the faint sound of laughter, shouting, and the bellowing of cattle could be heard through their open car windows. Horses nickered.

Jessy's heart began to pound as Lilli wheeled the roadster to a stop under a big elm tree. Was *he* one of the riders loping around? Jessy wondered. So many big hats, bright shirts. Any one of the lean, broad-shouldered men sitting so naturally in their saddles might be Hatcher Elroy. But no. Not yet. Jessy was sure, deep inside, she would recognize him in an instant. "It's a—this is a nice place," she told Lilli in a quavering voice as they climbed from the car.

Jessy and Lilli joined the others walking toward the home-made benches that edged an area of flat-beaten earth. Looking at the young farmwives in pretty print dresses, and older, sun-bon-neted women, Jessy saw several familiar faces. She'd seen these people on Ardensville streets and in the stores. If they had tele-phones, their voices doubtless would be even better known to her, and hers to them.

Without seeming to, Jessy continued to look hopefully from rider to rider. A cowboy dressed in black, on a big sorrel horse, caught her staring. He winked, swept off his wide-brimmed hat, and bowed low from the saddle. "'Mornin', ladies," he said, grin-ning.

Jessy looked quickly away. She almost lost her footing as a young boy, chased by another, bumped into her. She righted her-self, embarrassed when the cowboy chuckled, "Careful, Ma'am. We raise 'em wild out here." He rode away with a last tip of his hat.

Lilli caught her elbow and whispered from the side of her mouth, "Him? Was he your cowboy?" Jessy shook her head. Lilli sighed. "Fiddlesticks, he's real pretty."

They found places on the rough benches, smiled and said hello in answer to the shy, soft howdies from the other women. "Dusty, isn't it?" Lilli waved a small hand in front of her face and frowned as a group of racing youngsters stirred up dust in front of the benches.

Without half-trying she could find a lot wrong with this place, Jessy thought irritably. Noisy kids, dust, sticky flies. The smell of cows and horses so strong she could hardly breathe. And where was Hatch Elroy, anyway?

"John!" a woman directly behind her thundered at her child. "You stop that runnin', right now!"

A boy of about five skidded to a halt and fell in the dust at

Jessy's feet, his head missing the edge of the bench by a hair. Jessy reached out to help him to his feet. "Are you okay?" He wrenched from her grasp, snickered, and ran on, ignoring his mother's loud commands to come back.

"He's going to be the death of me," the woman in back of Jessy said.

From the corner of her eye, Jessy looked at Lilli and saw her fighting not to smile. As she was lowering her gaze from Lilli's, Jessy saw something else. A rider cantered out of the grove to their right, into the open. Jessy's breath caught. Hatch Elroy was here.

Sitting in the saddle on the pinkish-roan, Hatcher Elroy seemed taller than she remembered. The dark tan of his face and hands was a contrast to his deep blue shirt. Jessy couldn't see his eyes from so far, and hidden by his hat brim, but she knew they were bluer than the shirt. He rode out to join other men sitting their horses, talking, in the middle of the arena. Like he was part of the horse, Jessy thought. Like her horse-crazy little brother, Clay, rode.

Jessy considered telling Lilli that Hatch was here, then decided to wait. For now, Hatcher Elroy would be her own special secret. All at once, though, his face turned her way. Jessy's heart thumped so hard it seemed others could hear it.

Hatch's head jerked up, he turned his mount full around, facing Jessy. His finger touched his hat brim. So. He recognized her. Was he glad to see her here, or did she just imagine it? What if she hadn't come to this wonderful rodeo? All these nice people—beautiful day! Brimming with good feeling inside, Jessy squiggled up straight, beaming, ready to enjoy the rodeo.

A squatty cowboy on a sleek black horse cantered to the middle of the arena. He took off his hat and let it rest over the saddle horn. "Good mornin' folks!" he shouted. "We're mighty glad you came. We're here to ride bucking broncos, do some steer roping, and we'll have a horse race or two for you. We ain't big-time, but we got style, don't we boys?"

That brought a chorus of hooted denial and loud laughter from the riders ranging back and forth along the edge of the field.

"Awright, then," the announcer conceded, "we ain't got style. But we're gonna give these folks a durn good show, anyhow. Right?"

This time there was hearty agreement. Jessy and Lilli, along with others in the watching crowd, laughed and clapped their hands.

The bucking horse contest started the show. When it came time for Hatch Elroy to ride, Jessy squirmed to the edge of the bench. The horse he rode was an ugly, hammerheaded animal the cowboys called "Nightmare." Nightmare pitched and whirled like the paddles of a butterchurn until Jessy wanted to cover her eyes. She was sure Hatch would be thrown off. But he clung on, one hand flying free, until someone shouted, "Time! That's it. You rode 'im, Hatch!

Nightmare crow-hopped to a standstill. Hatch slid from the saddle, then ducked and ran when the horse whirled to kick him. A mounted rider took the dropped reins and led the kicking horse from the arena. Reaching the edge of the field, Hatch laughed and shook hands with another rider.

"Whew," Jessy breathed, and added without thinking, "I'm glad that's over." She was aware that Lilli turned to give her a curious stare, but Jessy pretended not to notice. She gave full attention, instead, to the event the announcer was explaining. Wild steer roping. In this contest, the squatty cowboy told them, a steer would be roped by a mounted cowboy, the noose to catch the steer's horns. The cowboy would get off his horse as fast as he could, wrestle the steer to the ground by the horns, then quickly tie three of the brute's legs together with a thong, all in a race against time. Tying done, the cowboy must throw his hands in the air to signal he was finished.

A while later, Lilli gasped, "Oh, no!"

Jessy saw it, too. A steer in the process of being tied broke free and hoisted rear-end first to its feet. The brute whirled on a dime, horns lowered to try and hook the startled cowboy. The cowboy, thankfully not Hatch, Jessy thought, leaped backward, lost his balance, then scrambled for his horse. He had no more landed in the saddle when a second cowboy, Hatch, roped the steer and urged it off the field.

Jessy clapped and clapped. She stopped when she realized she was the only one still applauding. Lilli was looking at her, a faint smile on her lips. Jessy lifted her chin and stared straight ahead.

Chapter 15

THE STEER PICKED for Hatch to rope and bring down looked like the wickedest of the lot, to Jessy. Her heart pounded as she watched Hatch's coil of rope sing out straight—the loop settling over the rocking-chair-sized horns. Hatch came off his horse on the run, grabbed the horns, dug in his heels and twisted, and the steer was down. On one knee, he took a leather thong from where he held it between his teeth and he whipped it about the animal's legs. People gasped as he jumped to his feet, his hands in the air.

"Best time," someone shouted, "that had to be the best time." Sounds of cheering, laughing, and hoarse shouts filled Jessy's ears. "Hoo, Hatcher, you done it, son." Jessy saw a silver-haired rancher slap Hatch on the back.

Horse racing filled another hour or two, and then the contests were over. A quiet time followed as the cowboys gathered to tally the best times to find out the winners.

Lilli reached over and patted Jessy's hand. Jessy tried to smile, but her chin shook. They left the bench, silently agreeing they were tired of sitting and needed a stretch. As soon as they were a few steps away from the crowd, by themselves, Lilli said, "I sat through that whole thing not saying a word, Jessamyn Faber. I heard your whimpers and gasps every time a certain rider looked like he might get hurt. I *know* who your cowboy is. He's the one in the dark blue shirt. The good-looking one riding over here."

Jessy took a quick look. Hatcher Elroy was coming toward them. No doubt about it. She waited, her mouth frozen in a crooked smile.

He drew the pink roan to a halt a few steps from Jessy and Lilli. "'Afternoon, Miss Faber." He looked at Lilli. "Ma'am." He removed his hat, showing a strip of white skin between his deep tan face and wavy brown hair. "Did you ladies enjoy the show?"

"The show was grand, I liked every minute of it," Lilli crowed, before Jessamyn could find her voice. "Did you win, Mr. Elroy?"

Hatch shrugged. "Nope, I didn't win the big purse. But I had a few best times, so I'm takin' home a few dollars." He looked directly at Jessy. "Our foolishness out there ain't so dangerous as it looks, if that's what you're thinkin', an' no worse'n what we go through on the ranch every week."

"You're a rancher?" Lilli piped, before Jessy could reply.

He shook his head. "I'm ramrod, foreman, for the Bar M, Tom Moorehouse's outfit. But I aim to have my own spread someday. Been workin' in that direction since I was a button kid. Got my first ranch job when I was thirteen, mostly shovelin'— well, shovelin'." He patted his shirt pocket. "I hang on to most of my winnings, and when it builds a mite, I take it and buy a few head of calves. Tom lets me run 'em with his stuff. Got a pretty good herd."

"That must please your wife and kids," Lilli said in wide-eyed innocence.

Jessy's face flamed. She'd like to kick Lilli for being so bold.

She couldn't look at Hatcher Elroy. "No wife, no kids," he said, "not that I'm against either—"

"If you haven't made special plans for a picnic dinner, Mr. Elroy," Lilli said, "would you join us? Jessy and I brought far too much food, and we'd love to share."

He looked at Jessy questioningly. Until that moment, she hadn't said a word. Both annoyed with Lilli for being forward, and yet glad Lilli had asked Hatch to eat with them, she added her own invitation, "Please do join us, Mr. Elroy." She took Lilli's arm. "And excuse my lack of manners. I'd like you to meet my good friend, Lilli Miller. Lilli, this is Hatcher Elroy."

"Hatch," he growled. "I'm glad for the invite, but call me Hatch." He dismounted. Leading the horse, he walked alongside Jessy toward the grove, and shade.

Jessy looked up and caught his eyes in a quiet appraisal of her. He grinned shyly. Jessy smiled back and hoped that her feeling inside didn't show in her face. "Y-you have a very nice horse," she murmured. "My little brother, Clay, would love your mare."

"Rainbow is a good little pony," Hatch commented, patting the horse's neck. "We been together a long time. I got a couple of her colts, good horses. You like horses, Jessy?"

"Yes, I do. We always kept horses on our place, at home. Nice animals, but not such good horses as I've seen today. Some of these are just beautiful; they look like show animals."

Hatch looked pleased. "Not everybody knows good horseflesh when they see it. Plains' horses are fine animals. And you won't find horses better cared for than in this country, either."

"Were the horses we saw today, and the cowboys, all from west Kansas?" Jessy asked as they reached Lilli's roadster.

"Both sides of the border," Hatch told her. "A lot of 'em from Colorado."

While the girls got the picnic basket and a blanket from the car, Hatch led his mare to a wagonload of hay, where other horses were tethered. Jessy spread the blanket on a patch of grass in the shade of a cottonwood. Lilli began taking sandwiches from the basket. "Hatcher Elroy is nice," Lilli said in a soft whisper. "The perfect man for you, Jessy."

"For goodness sake, Lilli," Jessy implored, "don't embarrass me anymore! Practically asking if he has a wife!"

"That's something you need to know from the start."

"I don't need to know! We're just friends, Lilli."

"*You* say."

"Shhh! He's coming back."

While others picnicked, two guitar players and a fiddler made music from a wagon. Jessy was glad the music kept Lilli entertained, her tongue stilled. Under the trees, talk was quiet, laughter soft.

When the meal was finished, the trio continued to listen to the music for a while, then Lilli jumped up. "I'm going to ask if they'll play, 'Oh! Susanna', so everybody can sing along." Off she flew. The song was played—cowboys and their womenfolk sang lustily, and the children danced. But Lilli didn't return directly, and Jessy knew she was leaving her alone with Hatch on purpose.

Jessy wished the day could go on forever. She might not see Hatch again for a long time. And back in Ardensville was the Klan and all of that....

Hatch asked, "Anything wrong, Jessy? You look kinda' sad. Something I can do? I did a pretty fair job, getting the leeches out of your foot that time."

She smiled and shook her head. "It's nothing. Just that I—I suppose because I've had such a good time today—I'd like it *not* to end." Then she worried, did that sound—all right? Seeing the look on Hatch's face, she felt better.

He told her, "I been tryin' to work up the courage to tell you one more time I'd like it fine if—if you'd let me come callin' on you. I know I'm just an ordinary cowpoke, but—can I see you again?"

"Yes," she said happily. "I'd like that. I should tell you though, that my free hours aren't the best. I'll try to work something out with my boss though."

For the next half-hour they talked freer, often interrupting each other, as though suddenly there were endless things each wanted to know about the other. Time flew.

Lilli came back. "Sorry, kid," she told Jessy, "but we're going to have to start back. It's a long drive, and it will be late when we get back to Ardensville as it is."

"I know." Jessy put their things back into the basket and folded the blanket. Hatch took them from her. They walked side by side to the roadster. Lilli trailed a few steps behind.

"There's a country dance comin' up soon," Hatch told Jessy. "I'd like for you to go with me. Don't know just when it's to be, but I'll let you know."

"Of course. I'll try to be free. Just call."

Hatch turned and said to Lilli, "Nice meetin' you, Miss Miller." He tipped his hat to Jessamyn. "S'long, till next time."

Jessy looked up at him for a long moment. "Good-bye, Hatch." And for not the first time turning away from him was hard to do. Her feet might have been planted in glue. Jessy bit her lip and got in the roadster.

"See you around, cowboy," Lilli quipped, "and thanks for a good show." She slid behind the wheel and started the engine.

Oriel Creek Campground was some distance behind them before either of them spoke. Lilli, looking over at Jessy, murmured a small, "Oh." She patted Jessy's arm. "Hon, you're crying. Don't do that."

"I am not crying."

"Your eyes are wet. From dust or something?"

"Oh, Lilli," Jessamyn confessed, "I'm having the dumbest feeling. I can't stand leaving him. It—it *hurts*. Now, isn't that stupid?"

Lilli didn't answer for a moment. When she did, her usual bantering tone was gone. "Love isn't stupid, Jess, it's the very best thing can happen to any of us. Don't fret, hon. I *know* you and

Hatch Elroy are meant for each other. He asked to see you again, didn't he?"

Jessy nodded. She wiped her eyes. "And I hope it's soon."

At the switchboard a few days later, Jessy plugged into the eighteen line. It was Etta Moorehouse, Hatch's boss' wife. "Central? Our Hatch wanted to call you himself, but he had to go out to the Brushy Creek range to check on some new calves. There's a dance over to the Tooney's, Saturday night. Hatch'd like to take you, and Tom and me want you two to have supper with us before you go to the dance."

"I won't have to—" Jessy started to say that she didn't have to work, she could get Gussie to work for her, but Mrs. Moorehouse interrupted.

"Now, you can't say no. There ain't a better young man anywhere than Hatcher Elroy, and he's taken a real shine to you, Central."

"I'd love to go to the dance, and thank you for the invitation to supper."

"Well, good! Miss Faber, I been wantin' to meet you personal, myself. Always felt if you are half as nice as your voice, you're a sweet girl. Hatch says that you are."

"Thank you," Jessy said, feeling herself color from the compliment. "If that's all, Mrs. Moorehouse, I'd better get off the line and go to work. Flaps are down all over my board. Tell Hatch I'll be happy to go to the dance with him."

"He'll be in Ardensville to pick you up in our Ford, around six. 'Bye, Central, it's been nice talking to you—as a person, not just gettin' a number."

"Good-bye."

✪

I DON'T HAVE ANYTHING pretty enough to wear to a dance with Hatch," Jessy told Cowboy, sitting, watching with head cocked as Jessy went through her clothes that night. She had to look her prettiest ever. For the third time, her glance went back to the white dress trimmed with lace and blue ribbons. Her prettiest. Her graduation dress. Almost a year ago, that was. Farley had drowned a few months before.

She hadn't wanted to go, hadn't wanted to take part in the graduation. But Mama and Papa wouldn't hear of her missing it. A nightmare, that day. Her classmates had acted so young and lighthearted and carefree. Not the way she felt. The Baxters, Farley's parents, told her she looked lovely and congratulated her. What had she told them? "Leave me alone, just leave me alone!"

Why had she behaved so shamefully? To those good people? Childless now, because of her. With shaking hands, Jessy took the dress from the hanger and held it up, her face hot with guilt. Maybe because there had been hard times, bad times, in her life before—Farley—but Mama and Papa had taken the brunt of them. Then it was as if she were almost grownup, *separate*, a person, who had to deal with Farley's death for herself, by herself. It was so hard…. She knelt to the kitten. "I'll wear the white dress," she told Cowboy around the lump in her throat, "and I'll do better. Please, don't give up on me."

Saturday night, Jessy opened the telephone office door after a firm knock sounded. Hatch stood there, hat in hand, his wavy hair still wet but neatly combed. He wore a pale yellow shirt; a deep orange scarf was knotted about his neck. His boots shone like glass. Jessy drew in a long breath, "Won't you come in?" she asked. "I want you to meet my boss. She's going to work for me the last few hours today."

"Lordy," he whispered for her ears only. "Lordy if you don't look like a dream, Jessy." He reached hesitantly to take her hand, as though if he touched her she might disappear. Jessy curled her fingers solidly about his, and it seemed to help him. He strode inside, hat in hand.

"Mrs. Stuberg, I'd like you to meet Hatcher Elroy. He's taking me out for the evening."

Gussie Stuberg turned and blinked. "My," she said, "My!" She dropped the cord she was holding and came off the stool, totally ignoring the switchboard. "He's handsome, Jessamyn! And a gentleman I can tell. After Mr. Munker"—Gussie sighed deeply—"a good-looking cowboy would be my second choice!" She saw Jessy look worriedly at the board. "Oh, them calls, most of 'em ain't no more important than a hill of beans, likely. They'll all be jumpin' down my throat, though." She actually curtsied for Hatch. "Nice to meetcha, Mr. Elroy. You take good care of Jessy. She's a fine girl, and I can't imagine how I'd do without her."

"I will, ma'am. If you're ready, Jessy"—he looked down at her—"we'd best be going. Etta will throw a fit if her chicken dinner burns, waiting on us. She said she wants everything just right for 'Central'."

HOW COULD TIME pass so fast? Jessy wondered as they parked the Ford in the Moorehouse ranchyard. She could remember hardly anything about the trip! Hatch's boss, a tall, thin man with a luxuriant mop of silvery hair and a drooping moustache, opened the door to them. "Come on in. Hatch, boy, bring your girl on in here so I can see her." Tom Moorehouse grabbed Jessy and hugged her as if she were a long-lost daughter.

Jessy laughed. "I remember seeing you at the rodeo, Mr. Moorehouse. And I guess I saw you once or twice at Mandy's, with Hatch."

"Tom!" he exclaimed. "You call me Tom. And this is my wife, Etta."

Gray, neat, and beaming, the ranchwoman came toward them. "Central, you're pretty as a picture, just the way I imagined you'd look. Tom, you bring 'em on to the table now. Everything's hot and ready. Don't hold back, Jessamyn," Etta said when they entered the dining room, "set right down over there next to Hatch.

And son, you go light on the biscuits tonight, I want your girl to have some. Tom, does that gravy look all right to you?"

Hatch chuckled. "Etta, stop fussing. You know darn well you set the best table in the country."

The older man reached out to hug his wife about the waist as she tried to bustle by him. "Come on, lovey, set down and enjoy your dinner." He raised the tall glass of milk that Etta had put in front of him. "Don't tell it around that an ornery old coyote like me drinks milk, Miss," he told Jessy. "I'd be laughed into the ground. But the truth is, I never developed a taste for the strong stuff."

"I won't tell," Jessy promised with a smile. Hatch winked at her and under the overhanging tablecloth her hand met his. She hoped he had an inkling of how much she liked Tom and Etta, how glad she was to be here with him tonight.

AGAIN, AT THE DANCE at the Tooney ranch five miles further down the road, Jessy told Lilli later, she was treated by Hatch's friends as though they had known her all their lives. "Such nice people. And the other cowboys, the older ranch owners and their wives—it's plain they like and respect Hatch." She was mentioning it again one day when Lilli said, "That was long ago. You've seen that cowboy at least five times since. What's happening?" They were having coffee at Mandy's. Lilli's elbows were on the table, her chin was propped in her hands. "Come on," she coaxed, "tell me what you see in that cowboy, him so ugly and all."

Jessy frowned in mock disbelief. "We both know Hatch is *not* ugly." She settled back to answer more seriously. "Hatch and I talk so easily to one another. About anything. Everything. Or we don't talk at all. We're happy holding hands, just being together. Oh, Lilli, I can't explain it—"

"You don't have to explain, kid," Lilli reached out to grasp Jessy's hands. "You're in love. It's written all over you, Jessy, and I am pea-green jealous."

"But you and Bill—?"

"He's been gone an awfully long time. I'd be scared he wasn't coming back at all, except that his car is at my place. I want him back." Lilli sighed. "Till then, I just load some more romance into the stories I'm working on. It isn't the same, but it's fun."

"Bill Washburn will be back, Lilli. Wait and see." Everything was so beautiful for her, it had to be for Lilli, too.

But Hatch Elroy wasn't the only thing Jessy had to think about though she wished he was. She couldn't pinpoint when Lombard Hale started talking to himself, words loose and disjointed, as he waited for his daughter, or someone else he was calling, to pick up the phone. Maybe he always had and she was just slow noticing it. But lately her attention was caught more than once by his ramblings. In one way it frightened her. She wondered if he was— sick. On the other hand, she'd heard that lots of people, perfectly sane and healthy, talked to themselves. She decided to ignore it.

Then one spring night, Jessy and Hatch were returning from a long buggy ride to watch the sun set, when a lone dark figure staggered up from the side of the road. Their horse veered, whinnying sharply. "Easy," Hatch shouted, pulling at the reins. "Whoa, now. Easy."

Jessy clutched the buggy seat with both hands, afraid the horse might still bolt and run with them. "What is it?" she whispered, when Hatch had the horse under control. "It looked like a man— something wrong with him."

Chapter 16

"I'LL SEE IF HE'S DRUNK," Hatch answered when they were stopped. "The guy fell down out there in the road." He gave the reins to Jessy to hold. "Stay in the buggy, hon."

In another moment, Hatch's voice carried softly back to her. "This man's hurt. Beaten up. Hold the horse quiet, honey. We're gonna take this fella to the Ardensville doc."

Jessy watched Hatch come toward her out of the shadows, carrying a still form. "He talked to me a mite, then he passed out cold," Hatch told her. "I'm gonna put him up here on the seat between us. Can you hold onto him, Jessy?"

"Sure, Hatch. Should we see if we can do something for him, ourselves, before we go on?" In a second, Hatch's match flickered and glowed bright. Jessy gasped. In spite of bruises and patches of blood on the swollen face, she recognized the man. "I know this man," she said in a stricken whisper. "His name is Isaac Burmann. He owns a department store in town."

Hatch swore softly under his breath. "Who'd do something like this to an old man?"

The Ku Klux Klan, Jessy thought silently, afraid to say so aloud. She'd been so happy lately, she had almost forgotten there was a Klan.

"I can't see that we can do a thing for him, here," Hatch added after a moment or two of examination. He blew out the match. "I know he's heavy on you, darlin', but do the best you can. We got to hurry. The poor old gent's face is gonna need stitches."

She rode in stiff, painful silence, both arms about the storekeeper, her feet braced on the buggy floor to keep from sagging. She shouldn't have urged Mr. Burmann to stay on. If he had sold out, after the Klan boycott began, left town, this wouldn't have happened. To go so far as *beating* a man!

"There's something more to this man's gettin' beat up, something that's troubling you, Jessy. I can feel it. Talk to me. Tell me what's going on. I want to know."

"Oh, Hatch, there's so much," Jessy confessed. "Terrible goings-on. Our—being together has been so nice. I kind of forgot every other thing. I had hoped I wouldn't have to talk about them."

"Honey, please. It'll help."

She began with the fire, which she still felt had been set at the Salonika children's shack on purpose. She told Hatch about the McGuires' two toddlers' mysterious disappearance and equally puzzling return, as if to scare their parents into leaving—or toe the line somehow. She talked about Klan parades and speeches, the cross burnings, the homes of so-called "undesirables" being pelted with rocks. She was sickened again, telling Hatch about the disgusting scene that took place at the Christmas Pageant.

"That was the Ku Klux Klan's first time out in the open, in Ardensville," she told him in a voice choked with feeling. "They've gotten bolder and bolder since then." Jessy drew a shuddering breath. "I'm sure the Klan did this, beat Mr. Burmann. His store window was broken one time, to scare him. He didn't want to go. All he wanted was to run his store in peace. Hatch, he wasn't hurting a soul!"

Once more Hatch swore under his breath. His free hand reached over to cover hers, holding Mr. Burmann. "Way out on the ranch we get behind on what's going on," he told her. "We heard rumors that some crazy people were acting up in Ardensville, told like a joke. But beating somebody up, fire—Jessy, has anybody else been hurt, before this?"

"I don't think so. But Hatch, there's lots of different kinds of hurt." Jessy told him about Lucian Salonika not being given jobs when he needed to work to feed and clothe his younger brothers and sisters. About stores in Ardensville going broke because of Klan-ordered snubs and boycotts. She explained how Joe Cooke had been barred from buying a business of his own. "All kinds of hurt, Hatch," she finished in a quiet voice, "and all of it rotten and unfair."

"Jessy, have those white-sheeted bums every done anything like that to you? If they even looked like they were gonna hurt you, I'd—"

"The mayor, who is very big in the Klan, I'm sure—I really think he's the leader—and I, don't see eye to eye. My friends are the same people he calls 'human garbage.' But I haven't been hurt. I suppose because the mayor feels sure I'll eventually come around to his way of seeing things."

"Hell!" Hatch thundered, "how can I take care of you. I'll be out on the range so much this summer. Our busiest time's comin' up. If anything, *anything* happened to you…! promise me, Jessy, if you ever need me at all, you'll ring Miss Etta, she'll know where I am. I'll come. Promise?"

"I promise, Hatch. But I'm sure I will be fi—" she broke off as Mr. Burmann moved slightly.

"No-o-o," the storekeeper moaned, "not—again."

Hatch whispered after a minute, "Are you okay, honey? Is he—all right?"

"He's not moving much. He's still again, but I can feel him breathing. Let's hurry, Hatcher."

"We're almost there. Listen, Jess, I'm takin' you home first. I don't want you with me when I take Mr. Burmann, here, to the doctor. No telling what them fools might try if they think you helped this gent. Poor old codger's been too far out to recognize you. I doubt he'll remember being picked up, even."

"It doesn't matter about that. Isaac Burmann is a good person. He'd protect me, if he did know I was here tonight."

A short while later, Hatch leaned across their injured passenger to kiss Jessy achingly on the lips. "You take care of yourself, honey," he whispered hoarsely as she climbed down from the buggy. "Lordy, you take care of yourself."

Two days after they'd found him beaten and bloody in the road, Isaac Burmann left Ardensville on the train west. Jessy heard the news at the switchboard. Her initial sadness turned to helpless anger. Why didn't someone do something? Did the Klan have its hooks into everybody in town? Sick at heart, she overheard further snatches of gossip about the incident: Isaac Burmann went out west because of bad health. His store had been bought by Lombard Hale, who would probably run it better, anyway.

Key open, ready to interrupt with an argument in Mr. Burmann's behalf, Jessy would again see the storekeeper's bruised and swollen face, his beard caked with blood. A shaking fear that the same thing could happen to her ended it. Knowing the Ku Klux Klan got its power in just this way—scaring people by example—was no help.

Poor Mr. Burmann. She hoped he was faring better wherever he was. He deserved better. Wishing him well in her heart was the most she could do for him, now.

One day, putting through the connection from the Hale automobile agency to his home, Jessy's ears caught the word, "Burmann." She hesitated the slightest second before ringing Hale's home phone number, and she heard him say, "gone." Jessy wished

Anna Cora would hurry and pick up the phone as she rang, again and again. Hale mumbled to himself, gibberish, then clearly, he said, "Joe Cooke, too, tonight." The mayor laughed to himself. Jessy shrank back on her stool, her blood running cold in her veins.

"Hello? Hello? Is it you, Daddy?" Anna Cora interrupted his chuckle.

"It's me, pumpkin. How are you doing, Annie? Has Mrs. Pierce been by to fit you for your new spring dresses? Tell her your daddy wants you to have four or five pretty dresses, now, you tell her—" Jessy closed the key on his voice with icy fingers.

Was Lombard Hale, the Ku Klux Klan, planning to do tonight to Joe Cooke and his sons what they had done to Mr. Burmann? It had to be stopped. But it shouldn't be up to her. Why didn't Ardensville have a police department! She supposed she could call the county sheriff. Jessy sighed. What would they say to her if she told them that the words, "Joe Cooke, too, tonight" were proof that something terrible was about to happen? They would think she was balmy. If only Mr. Burmann hadn't gone so soon; if he was here, he could tell the county sheriff what had happened to him. Then what she had to tell might mean something.

Hatch. But no, he was so far away, working. What if she called him to Ardensville, and it turned out to be nothing? On the other hand, she couldn't ignore what she'd heard. Jessy bit her lip, close to tears, and with a small balled fist, she pounded the curved edge of the switchboard. What was she supposed to do?

Lilli, she decided. Lilli could help her figure out what to do, if anything.

The day passed, and by the time she talked to Lilli that night, Jessy was calmer. She could even laugh. "You're supposed to be the one with the wild imagination," she said. "But look what I've cooked up in my little brain. It's hogwash, don't you think? Nonsense, really?"

"I wish I thought so. But I don't. I bet a dollar to a doughnut that Ardensville's ghost bunch is planning mischief or worse for Joe Cooke tonight."

"But we can't be sure," Jessy argued. "What can we do? I don't want Joe hurt, like Isaac Burmann, but—" At the look of surprise on Lilli's face, Jessy realized her friend didn't know about the beating. Hatch had begged her to stay out of it, but now Jessy told her friend everything.

"Jessy, you should have told someone, you should have called the police. Didn't Hatch? Or the doctor?" She shook her head. "Mr. Burmann might have talked Hatch out of it, or maybe Hatch left it up to the doctor. And the doctor"—Lilli's voice dropped—"probably belongs to the Klan. And now Mr. Burmann is gone." She looked at Jessy. "Kid, we can't let this happen again."

"But we're not Belle Starr and Calamity Jane." Jessy tried to ease the tension with a joke. "We can't go after 'em with guns drawn." She added, more seriously, "Lilli, the Klan is big, and dangerous."

Lilli mused, "It worked, beating up Mr. Burmann. He left town. The Klan's probably busting their buttons with pride about that. Now they'll push even harder to make this a one-color, one-religion, single-minded, very dull town."

"It's getting late." Jessy stood up. "I haven't had supper."

"Hold on a second!" Lilli cried. She paced. "Wait. I think I know what we can do, kid, the two of us."

Jessy cringed inside. "Lilli, no. Not us, you and me. If you think we can do something about the Klan, forget it, we can't. I promised Hatch, anyway."

Lilli, fairly dancing about her parlor with excitement, paid no attention. "I know, I know what we can do." She pointed a finger at Jessy, "Go to Mandy's and buy a cake, any cake, and bring it back here. There isn't much time. I'll get everything else ready while you're gone."

"What are you talking about?"

"A party. A birthday party for Joe Cooke. Tonight."

"Lilli, whatever you're thinking, it won't work."

"Yes it will. Always before the Klan has had the upper hand because they catch people by surprise. This time we know ahead of time, so we can turn the tables on them."

Jessy floundered. "H-how?"

"We're going to be there when they come, and we're going to make them look foolish." She waved a hand impatiently at Jessy. "Go on, hurry. Ask Gussie to work awhile, late, for you. I'll tell you more, later."

Jessy felt foolish when she found herself slipping along the street like a Mata Hari to Mandy's. She felt guilty a few minutes later, asking Gussie to work for her. Because Gussie liked Hatch so much, she readily agreed to switch hours, give Jessy more time, any time she asked. Jessy didn't go into detail about the "party."

When she got back with the cake, she told Lilli, who met her at the door carrying a small bundle, "This is dumb and sneaky and I want us to call it off."

Lilli pushed her back out onto the porch and closed and locked the door. "Is it dumber, or sneakier, than what the Klan does?" she asked.

"I guess it isn't," Jessy admitted lamely. Truthfully, she wished she hadn't told Lilli anything at all about tonight. "I'm scared," she whispered aloud.

"We won't be hurt," Lilli said staunchly, grabbing Jessy's hand to pull her down the steps. "And we can help Joe. I know we can."

"He's going to think we're addlepated."

"Not when we explain."

Joe's house was near the railroad tracks. Jessy had seen his boys playing in the yard a few times and knew they kept an old horse and a few chickens. The inside of the house, when they got there, was sparsely furnished but tidy.

Like Lilli, Joe Cooke didn't seem to doubt that the Ku Klux Klan planned to attack him. Jessy's last shred of hope that she and

Lilli were mistaken vanished as Joe nodded sadly. The lines in his face deepened. "They won't give up; they won't ever give up no matter what," he said. "I have kep 'my place' as Mr. Hale told me to. I haven't forced the issue of my owning the livery. I could have hired a lawyer and fought back. I said nothing when they made my boys feel so bad at that Christmas doings, although I would gladly kill for my sons if I thought it would help. What does Mr. Hale, the Klan, want? Why is the color of my skin such a threat, when I follow their wishes to the letter. Nothing suits them, nothing." Jessy thought she saw a flash of anger in his eyes, but it was gone so quickly she couldn't be sure.

"Where are your boys tonight?" she asked, realizing she hadn't seen them.

"Edwin and Harry are in the back room studying their books. If there's going to be a fuss, I better warn them now, so they won't be scared."

It was not knowing what was going to happen that made her feel so scared, Jessy realized. There were chill bumps on her flesh, and she moved about woodenly to help Lilli set up their "party." Joe was in his sons' room a long time. "I think they understand," he said when he returned, "but it's hard for me to tell them this thing."

The girls nodded in sympathy. Lilli brushed a crumb from the edge of the cake plate, and Jessy saw that her hand was shaking. In that same moment, Jessy heard a sound outside. She listened and heard a muffled thump, a soft chuckle. She looked at Lilli, at Joe, and drew in a long, quivery breath. "Someone's outside," she whispered.

"They're here," Lilli agreed in a small voice. Her eyes were unusually large in her pale face. "I wonder if they'll come to the door, or what?"

They waited. Jessy heard a horse snuffle. She thought she heard a car engine purr to a stop. A man coughed, and a second guttural voice gave a command. She could hear creaking leather, thudding hoofs and the blowing of several horses.

The Klan was not very secret at this. Someone outside laughed. Maybe these sounds were meant to be heard, she thought, to add to the victim's fright. It was undoing her, certainly. Jessy caught her lip between her teeth, bit hard, and waited.

Icicles chased up and down her spine. She couldn't stand it, the waiting, any more, not any more! Jessy raced to the door and yanked it open. "Surprise!" she shouted with all her might. "Surprise!" All of Jessy's tenseness went into the shout. With it done, she felt better. It wasn't exactly what they had planned to do, Jessy realized, shaking, but it was done. Lilli, cake in hand, hurried to join Jessy in the open doorway.

The yard was filled with white-robed figures on horseback. One of them, on foot, separated from the others and started toward the barn where Joe kept his horse. Jessy looked hard at the sheeted figure. From the man's uncommon way of walking she was sure it was Cecil Kinglake.

"That's Cecil," Lilli echoed her thought in a whisper. "He's got something. It looks like a coal oil can."

"They are going to burn my horse, Molly," Joe said from where he watched at a dark window. "They can't do that!"

She'd rather be anyplace else but here, Jessy was thinking, shivering. But she was tired, too, of being a wishy-washy, helpless good-for-nothing. She grabbed the cake from Lilli's hands and made three jerky steps out onto the porch. "Wait," she called, trying to muster a friendly tone although it was hard to speak at all. She motioned at the halted figure, which was only steps away from the barn, now. "Come in pl-please. It's Joe's birthday. Won't all of you please come in and celebrate with us? Come in, have some birthday cake and coffee."

Leather and harness creaked as men shifted in their saddles. There was uneasy laughter as they turned shrouded heads to look at one another, and then, to a black automobile Jessy saw parked behind them. She felt a spurt of relief that she and Lilli had at least managed to put this small wrinkle in the Klan's plans.

"Hey, it's old Imperial Wizard or What's Doodle, himself," Lilli whispered as a white form got out of the car and strode forward.

Chapter 17

"HERE IS AN EXAMPLE of what is infecting our community," the leader shouted. Lombard Hale, Jessy was sure of that voice. "The very thing we have to prevent. Two young girls consorting with a black man! You see it. All of you see this, don't you? The girls are young. Out of ignorance they may not know how white girls should behave. But the nigger, he knows better. He must be taught—"

Jessy stumbled as Lilli pushed around in front of her, yelling, "Don't you call me ignorant, Lombard A. Hale, you yellow-bellied coward!" She stomped her foot. Jessy heard her sob. "I recognize your voice. That sheet is no disguise for the likes of you, Mr. Mayor." Jessy tried to restrain Lilli, tried to pull her back. "I don't care," Lilli sobbed to her, "look who's calling who ignorant."

Lilli tore from Jessy's grasp and charged to the first step. Hands on her hips, she shouted, "Come on Mr. Hale, you Whang Kloggle or whatever you are, bring your friends inside. Take off your sheets and let's talk like real people. If you proud fellows think you're so right, then you won't mind showing your faces, will you?"

Jessy's legs felt like mush but she had no choice but to join her friend. "I recognize your voice, too, Mr. H-Hale. And others out there, I know you. From the way you move, from your size." She drew a deep breath to try and halt the quivering in her voice. "I just w-want to tell you this: Joe Cooke is a gentleman, a kind person. He lives quietly here with his boys. Has he ever done a single thing to harm any of you? Honestly, what you are here to do—makes no sense."

"Throw the match!" Jessy didn't recognize the voice filled with excitement and anticipation.

"Oh, don't," she pleaded. She watched Hale's erect sheeted figure march about. He spoke to first one mounted white form, then another, and a third. The hooded men shook their heads in turn and backed their mounts. Were they leaving? They had rejected Hale's command, whatever it was. He moved, so agitated his sheet fluttered and swished. Then he motioned to Cecil King-lake, who still stood holding the coal oil can.

Cecil stayed where he was. Lombard Hale stormed toward him and muttered a threat that Jessy couldn't make out. Cecil put the can down on the ground. He started toward the porch, where Jessy, Lilli, and Joe watched and waited.

The handyman moved slow, his pockets jangled eerily. Twice he looked back over his shoulder. Each time the mayor motioned him to keep going. With heavy feet Cecil took the steps one by one. Jessy wanted to run, but stood frozen. Cecil came toward her. He hesitated, lifted his hand, dropped it, then lifted it again. A tear rolled unchecked down Jessy's cheek. As desperately as she wanted to, she still could not move.

"Cecil," Lilli said behind her, "Cecil, don't. You know me, we've worked together, we're friends."

A kind of shudder seemed to pass through the big man. He

snatched the cake from Jessy, halted the slightest second, then he pushed it into her face. Jessy had no time to cry out, she felt smothered. She heard Cecil's whimper before he shoved her, hard. Her skull cracked against a post as she went down, blinded from the cake. For a second the wind was knocked out of her; Jessy choked and gasped. She lay on the porch, dazed but conscious, wiping at her eyes.

In her ears Lilli sobbed furiously. Joe's voice begged, "Stop, stop! Go away. You shouldn't hurt these girls. If it's me you wa—" Through a blur Jessy saw a sheeted form leap to the porch and shove lumbering Cecil aside. The new man's heavy fist struck the side of Joe's head. The black man crashed to the floor beside her.

"You didn't need to do that," a voice she didn't know, out in the yard, growled. Jessy pulled herself up to a sitting position. They were going; she saw the sheeted figures turn their horses. Another voice muttered, "Picking on girls. Shoot. I feel like two cents."

The car engine churned to life; the automobile backed down the lane, horses and riders followed.

Warm tears coursed down Jessy's cheeks. She sobbed uncontrollably. Why did this awful thing have to happen? For several minutes sobs continued to wrack her body. She covered her wet face with her hands and wished she could stop crying. Then finally Lilli took her hands down and wiped at the lumps of frosting her tears hadn't washed away.

"Poor kid, poor Jess," Lilli crooned. "They've gone. Don't cry."

"Is she all right?" Jessy heard Joe ask. "Is she hurt bad?"

"Can we have a glass of water, Joe? We'll get her to take a drink. She's all right." Lilli's fingers gently pushed Jessy's hair out of her eyes. "Come on, stop with the tears before you wash us all away in the flood." She took Jessy's chin in her hand. "Take a deep breath," she ordered. "Take another one, another. Here we are. Joe brought you some water, Jessy. That's it. Drink up. Good."

"I-I'm sorry," Jessy gasped in another minute. She shook her head frantically and took a deep breath when she felt the tears start again. "I've never been so—so scared in all my life. It was terrible. They…." she looked down and brushed crumbled cake from the front of her dress.

"You didn't look scared to me; you did good," Lilli told her.

Jessy weaved to her feet with Lilli's help. Her head still hurt. "I want to go home. Let's go home, Lilli."

"All right, kid."

"I'll go with you girls."

"No, Joe," Lilli told him, "we'll be all right. They won't try to hurt us."

"*You* can say that," Jessy lamented. "Cecil Kinglake didn't give you a frosting facial. You didn't get slugged like Joe did, either."

"Jess, you are all right, aren't you?" Lilli was cheerful. "Your ladylike pride is a bit damaged, maybe, but otherwise? And Joe, aren't you okay?"

"I hit my head when I fell, but it doesn't hurt so much now," Jessy admitted.

"I've been hit harder," Joe said.

Jessy looked at him. "Mr. Cooke, wouldn't you be better off somewhere else? If you have the money, why don't you just leave Ardensville?"

"To some *nigger* section of a big city?" he asked. "Another small town with somebody like Lombard Hale running it? There's so many like him, they could have all been cut from the same cloth." His glance fastened on the porch post. "Maybe I could hit it lucky in another little town somewhere. Truth is, I'm tired of looking."

"What's happening in Ardensville is happening all across the United States," Lilli agreed solemnly. "Listen, Jess," she put an arm around her, "at least *some* of those guys were ashamed of tonight's shenanigans. That's what we wanted! It is a beginning. We can all sleep better tonight."

Maybe Lilli slept fine, Jessy thought next day, but she hadn't.

"It's the end for me in Ardensville," Jessy told Lilli when they met for lunch. "I'm going back to The Ranch."

Lilli's shoulders sagged. "You're not, kid, really?"

Jessy toyed with the salt and pepper shakers in front of her. "My sister Willow's baby is due any day. They can use me there. Lombard Hale can have this town for all I care, have it any way he pleases. It doesn't take much to scare me, Lilli," she admitted. "The goose egg on the back of my head is enough."

Lilli's voice was cool and steady. "If that's what you want. But think about this Jessy: the Klan can be beaten if it's faced down. But if people don't do something, Klan rule will soon be strong everywhere. There won't be any place to run to. What are they under those sheets," she asked, "but ordinary people. Some of them cruel, a lot of them ignorant and misguided, like poor Cecil."

"I'm going," Jessy persisted. "I just can't stand it, Lilli. I like things peaceful, quiet. I thought that's what this town was, when I came here. Anyway, please understand. That's the way I am, I can't help it. I hate trouble."

"I don't like reminding you, Jessy, but aren't you running away from something that happened back home, too?"

She looked away from Lilli's set jaw. What could she say? "I—I'm all right about th-that."

"Tell you what." Lilli's mood lightened suddenly. "We'll both go away. I've been wanting to get back to St. Louis. Come with me. It'll be fun, exciting. What do you say?"

"Why don't you leave me alone? You know you're teasing, Lilli Miller. And I can do what I please!"

"Sure you can. *You* can. But the Salonika kids can't. They have to do what the Klan orders. Maybe leave town whether they want to or not. Or, if they stay much longer, one of them, maybe all, will be hurt. Others, too. Joe, his boys. Like Isaac Burmann, they'll *have* to go. This isn't their town, our town. It's Lombard

Hale's. Okay. Go back to your precious Faber Ranch. While you're at it, give up the best thing that's ever happened to you, too: Hatch Elroy. He can't be expected to ride two hundred miles on Saturday nights to see you, you know."

"Stop, Lilli." Jessy looked at the wall for several minutes. "You make me feel so ashamed," she admitted, finally. "And I can't leave Hatch. Why do you have to always be so smart, Lilli?"

Lilli's eyes started to glisten. "I know we ought to see this through. Do what we can to help make Ardensville a decent place to live for anybody who chooses to live here. But it beats me what to do next. I just don't know."

They sat in silence several minutes. Jessy took a sip of her tea, now warm. "If I—I stay," she wavered finally, "I think there is s-something I can do. When I first overheard Lombard Hale mention Joe, and I guessed what the Klan was up to, I got an idea—no, it's crazy. Forget it," she changed her mind. "It wouldn't work."

"Tell me, anyway, Jess!" Lilli implored.

She shook her head slowly. Lilli wouldn't give her any rest, though, till she told her. "Hale talks to himself while he waits for me to ring whatever number he's calling," she told Lilli. "That's how I found out about the Klan attack on Joe, remember? The mayor mumbles to himself a lot. I might hear about other Klan doings, if I listened. I—I might find out things from other callers, Klan members, too, if I paid more attention." Her shoulders fell. "I hate to eavesdrop, though, I really do. There may even be some law against it. But if I could learn things, we could warn people ahead of time, and they could be ready."

"Fantastic!" Lilli's eyes danced. "What else? I can tell by the look on your face, kid, that you've got more figured out." She leaned forward.

"If I had a secret signal," Jessy motioned nervously, "it might be that I could pass it along to the family who is going to be hit. The signal would be a—a password or something that I would work into a telephone conversation."

"Jessy, this plan is so wild"—Lilli grinned with delight—"it could have been mine. Go on!"

Jessy managed a faint smile. "Well, like I said, this message could be buried in other talk, innocent stuff. People will be listening in, they always do. Some of the eavesdroppers will be Klan members." She shivered and frowned. "It doesn't matter. Let's forget it, Lilli. It's a stupid idea, and I don't have the nerve to do it, anyway."

"What a pansy!" Lilli yelped.

"Shhh," Jessy cautioned, "people are looking at us. Anyway, I'm not a pansy, I'm a morning glory flower. My sister, Willow, always claimed she was a sturdy sunflower kind of person and I was a frail morning glory who hides from the heat—or problems, trouble."

Suddenly, Lilli's eyebrows shot up. "That's it!" she cried, ignoring the stares of the other diners. Jessy frowned, and Lilli lowered her voice. "Morning glory is a perfect password. You could work the words *morning glory* into a line or two of talk, and the person would know they are about to be hit. And the *time* for it, you'd have to get that in, somehow." Lilli looked thoughtful.

Jessy spoke up, "I could say things like, "It's glorious this *morning*; it won't be so nice *tonight*, though."

"It would work!" Lilli giggled softly. "Let's do it!"

"No," Jessy shook her head. "We've just been playing a silly game, and you know it, Lilli. Forget it."

"I should say not," Lilli argued. "We have to work out more of it. Like, we know *who* the obvious targets of the Klan will be—the foreigners who live here, the Catholics, and so on. They have to be told the plan so they'll know when you pass the secret warning what it's all about. That will be my job. I'll let the right people know about this."

"Lilli, I don't think—"

"You have to at least *try*, Jessy. Granted, it sounds like something little kids would cook up. But if we save some people from getting hurt, wouldn't it be worth it? C'mon, kid, let's give it a try. Somebody has to make a move to stop the Klan."

"A-all right. I will. But I'm going to be sorry," Jessy lamented. "I may not hear anything. But if I do, I'll try to...." She'd read something once, about going into battle armed with a feather. That's how she felt. "I'll do what I can."

Two letters came for Jessy in the mail next day, and she temporarily put everything else from her mind. Willow's handwriting was on the blue envelope. She decided to read her sister's letter first and save Hatch's for last. Walking home from the post office, she opened the blue envelope.

Willow wrote:

Dear Sis,

You have a niece, and you should see her. Chelanne Evans is the world's most beautiful, most precious baby. When are you coming to see us? Make it soon!

Love,
Willow

Jessy's heart lurched, reading the note. She closed her eyes and pictured the joy and excitement there'd be on The Ranch, and at Willow's. She was missing out. She'd write and tell Willow she'd be home as soon as she could, and then she'd work to make it happen.

How she missed them, all of them at home. And Hatch, she wished he could meet her family. She touched the cowboy's letter to her lips, then opened it. Reading the brief message, she felt a sharp disappointment.

Sweetheart,

I can't get in to see you this Saturday. Can't even get to a phone. We're plumb in over our heads, branding. Saturday two weeks from now I'll be there or else.

Is everything all right in town? Are them Klan buggers be-
having? If they ain't, the branding can go to hell, and I'll come.
Let me know.

Yours,
Hatch

It would be awful not to see Hatch for so long. But she was
not about to tell him about the ruckus at Joe's.

In the following days, it was like she was coming down with
something; Jessy felt listless and unhappy, she missed Hatch so
much she hurt. With little enthusiasm for the task, she listened
whenever Lombard Hale made a telephone call through the
board. As far as she could tell, there was nothing.

Then one morning, Lilli made an urgent call from the boarding house, insisting they meet at Mandy's on Jessy's noon break.

Chapter 18

AS SOON AS THEY had ordered sandwiches, Lilli leaned forward. "It's time to use our password." She took a nervous sip of ice water. "The McGuire family are going to have trouble again. Tonight."

"Lilli, are you sure you aren't imagining things?" Lilli's intense look showed that she enjoyed this cloak and dagger stuff.

"You'd better listen." Lowering her voice, Lilli said, "I was walking home from the grocery store a few minutes ago and I saw Lombard Hale arguing with Anna Cora. *Arguing.* You know how he is about her most of the time."

Jessy nodded, but she didn't say anything.

"I heard Anna Cora beg her father, 'Don't make Cecil go with you tonight, Papa, not to the McGuires'. A fire is bad. Cecil, or somebody else, might get hurt.' She was really worked up," Lilli said. "When I passed them, Hale tried to shush her. She started to cry, Jessy. And Hale mumbled something about '...just the coal shed to teach a lesson.' Then he hurried Anna Cora away, down the street."

Jessy felt numb. "Did you tell the McGuires what you heard?" she whispered.

"Can't. Hale saw *us* at Joe's, remember? He knows what side we're on. I kind of hummed to myself when I walked by them, and I hope he thinks I didn't hear anything. If I was seen going to the McGuires, he'd know I did and they'd do it some other time probably. Some time when we wouldn't know. You can't go tell them, either. But through your switchboard, Jessy, using the secret message, you can warn them!"

Jessy wavered. "Are you sure about what you heard, Lilli?"

"Absolutely positive. And we have to do something. Make the call, kid."

"I wish someone else…" Jessy began. "Shouldn't we call the county sheriff this time?"

"And accuse somebody of a crime that hasn't happened? Everything is too sketchy for that," Lilli reminded her.

"All right. I'll try to decide how to work the words 'morning glory' into a halfway sensible conversation. I sure hope the McGuires know what I'm doing."

"They'll know," Lilli assured her. "I managed to make the rounds late one night when I wouldn't be seen. Right after we cooked this up, I told everybody what they needed to know. Don't think I missed anyone."

Back at work, Jessy handled calls automatically. For some time she put off making the warning call, worried that she might give everything away to the wrong people.

Plugging into a line, later, she was startled to recognize Mrs. McGuire's voice, asking, "Central, will you ring the Jorgensens for me?"

Jessy's mind swam. What marvelous good luck! "How are you, Mrs. McGuire?" she asked, trying to sound casual. "Isn't this a lovely day? It's going to be warm, though." She thought fast.

"Our—our morning glories and petunias, of course, will need lots of *water. Water*," she repeated. "Hope it cools off by tonight, don't you?" She took a breath. "I'll ring Jorgensens for you."

"Wait," she heard Mrs. McGuire say softly at the other end. A silence seemed to go on forever. Then Mrs. McGuire replied, "Morning glories do take lots of water, when it's hot."

She understood! Jessy could have cried in relief and surprise that it worked. She'd done it. Whatever happened now was up to others.

Jessy didn't sleep sound that night. At any minute, she expected a pounding at the door to announce a fire. Nobody came; the night passed. Had the morning glory warning worked then? She wasn't very surprised when Lilli dashed in during the afternoon.

"It worked, Jess. You did it!" Lilli danced a quick jig and hugged Jessy, almost pulling her off the stool. "The McGuires were ready when the Klan got there."

"What happened?" Jessy laughed at Lilli's excitement.

"Mama and Papa McGuire and all nine kids were armed with buckets and dishpans and tubs of water," Lilli crowed. "The Klan rode up to their yard about midnight. But the white robed nincompoops didn't get to strike a match. Mrs. McGuire *thought* she saw a spark." Lilli giggled. "She yelled for the whole family to throw their water. They soaked the Ku Kluxers, kid. Oh, I wish I could have been there."

"How'd you find out about it, Lilli?"

"Mary Lewis, one of my permanent boarders, is a friend of Mrs. McGuire. Mary found out about it this morning. And, Jessy, people are laughing! Making jokes about all the sheets on clotheslines around town today, and it not being Monday washday, either. Things like that. You know, I think we may have more friends than we thought."

"It sounds good, Lilli," Jessy admitted. "But we were lucky this time. It might not go this way again."

"Jessy, don't give up. If it worked once, it will work again. Just stop and think what you accomplished. By saying those few words, you prevented a fire, maybe kept people from getting hurt."

Lilli was right. Jessy smiled. "I am glad I did it."

"And you know you have to keep warning folks," Lilli said, "at least until we can figure something else out."

A few days later, Jessy placed a call for Lombard Hale to Mr. Pierce at the drugstore. Possibly busy with customers, Mr. Pierce didn't pick up the phone at the first ring, or the second. Hale began to mumble to himself. The back of Jessy's neck prickled. "Slick Italian," she heard him hiss. "Surprise guests at Garibaldi's card party. Wilford can get our friends together—" Jessy shoved the key closed.

But what if someone was going to get hurt? She opened the key. "Mr. Hale," she asked, "did Mr. Pierce answer?"

"No, Miss Faber. Ring him again, please."

This time, Jessy stayed on the line, feeling both fear and guilt. Her heart pounded loud in her ears, but she managed to catch the words she needed to know, "—the boys tonight," the mayor whispered to himself, "we'll rough up that sinning wop—"

Jessy sat trembling. Lilli'd told her that the Klan was against immoral acts as well as everything else. Mama and Papa didn't hold with card playing, either, but they wouldn't think anyone had a right to go into someone's home, break things up, and tell the people what they could and couldn't do.

Feeling cold all over, but committed, Jessy rang the Garibaldi residence and waited for an answer. "Mrs. Garibaldi?" She sat up straighter. "This is Central. I just wanted to tell you that the paint you've been wanting, *morning glory* blue, is in now at the hardware. You might want to pick it up *tonight*."

Mrs. Garibaldi let out a faint shriek, then more calmly, said, "Thank you, Central. Thank you."

As usual, Lilli had the inside track on what happened, and before Jessy could tell her about the warning she'd sent, Lilli came to tell her, "Rose and Marco Garibaldi canceled their party. They were sitting home alone listening to Rudy Vallee singing on the radio when the Klan got there, charging up real ferocious to the Garibaldi's door. I heard that some of the Klan was awful disappointed when they found nothing 'immoral' in progress. They wanted to bust things up anyway. But they didn't. They just rode off like dogs with their tails between their legs."

"Besides the Ku Klux Klan and the Garibaldis, I thought I would be the only one to know about this." Jessy shook her head in perplexity.

"With your job, you should know that there aren't many secrets in a town as small as Ardensville, Jessy."

She nodded. "True. And it's only a matter of time before Hale and the Klan find out it's *me* who's warning people."

Lilli hugged her. "You can't quit, kid. Folks are beginning to see that the Klan's violence is directed toward dangers that are mostly imaginary."

A few moments later they parted.

Saturday morning, Etta Moorehouse called Jessy to tell her that Hatch still could not get away to come into town. Another week without seeing him? How could she get through it?

She didn't often go to the movies, except with Hatch on Saturday night, but on Tuesday evening Jessy decided she would go, to help pass the time until she could be with Hatch again. At the Orpheum's entrance, Jessy was surprised to see Lombard Hale coming toward her, a wide smile on his face. Something in his look caused her to tremble; her throat dried. As she turned toward the ticket stall, the mayor stepped in front of her. He tipped his gray felt hat, "My"—his voice was silk—"wasn't this a lovely *morning glory* day, my dear?"

Jessy could hardly keep from screaming. He bowed and chuckled and moved on down the street.

He knew! He knew what she'd been up to and why! Jessy groveled in her purse for money, threw it at the ticket girl, blindly grabbed the ticket offered her and ran down the aisle in the dark theater and fumbled into a seat. He knew.

She stared unseeing at the moving figures on the screen and listened to the piano playing background music for close to two hours. For several minutes after the movie was ended, Jessy sat. Then, cold clear through, she ran from the theater.

She let herself into the telephone office next door and locked the door. Now that Hale knew, would she be next on the Klan's list? Or did Hale know that by scaring her senseless, she wouldn't try anything else?

How had she gotten herself into this mess, anyway? It was Lilli's fault. No, it was her own. Jessy sat on the edge of her cot, with Cowboy in her lap, too gripped by fear to cry. A sudden knock on the telephone office door sent Jessamyn to her feet as though she'd been yanked by a cord. She stood frozen. Tears started down her cheeks. Were they here? Had the Klan come for her, finally? With tar, whips, a match?

A muffled, faraway voice spoke, "Central, I need to talk to you." It sounded like Cecil Kinglake. Jessy tiptoed from her room to look. The large shadowy figure outside was Cecil. She went to grasp the doorknob and turned it. Cecil Kinglake was alone, wearing his ordinary clothes, no sheet. In a sheet he would be the Klan's tool; as himself she was sure she could trust him.

"I—I'm sorry, Central," Cecil said, staring at her damp cheeks. "I didn't mean to sc-scare you."

Jessy attempted a smile. "Wh-what do you want? Is it an emergency? Did someone else, Mr. Hale, send you?" He shook his head hard, *no.* "C-come in, and let's sit down. You did give me a scare." She found the extra stool for Cecil and sank down on hers in front of the quiet switchboard. "Why did you come?"

Worry had replaced his usual happy expression. He wagged his shaggy blond head. "I come, I come to tell you. Before Mr. Hale—he knows the morning glory secret." Cecil moaned softly as though about to cry. "Anna Cora said I had to come and tell you."

Jessy admitted quickly, "I know he knows, Cecil."

"You do?" Cecil looked amazed. "Only this afternoon I told him." He wrung his big hands. "Anna Cora's daddy made me tell him all about it. I didn't want to—"

"But how did you know about the warning plan, the secret words, morning glory?"

A sweet smile lit Cecil's face. He spoke proudly, shoulders erect. "Anna Cora told me. She's so smart. Lots of people think she's simple. Like me. But Annie is smart, she—she likes to listen on her phone to other people talkin'. An', an' she kept hearing people say stuff about morning glories, you know?"

"I'm afraid I know," Jessy said, blushing.

"After people talked about morning glories," Cecil was saying, "our Klan club would have trouble. Every time," he said wonderingly. "Anna Cora's Papa would be riled! Because we couldn't surprise people anymore."

Jessy nodded sympathetically, hiding the fear she felt, and waited for Cecil to go on.

"Mr. Hale blamed me," Cecil told her. "He said it was me tattling, going around telling people where our club, the Klan club, was going to visit next time. Anna Cora knew it wasn't me. She said to tell her papa it wasn't me. Central, I *had to* tell him it was the morning glory words on the telephones that got people ready for us. Mr. Hale says you're a troublemaker; he doesn't like you anymore. I'm sorry I told on you, Central." His pale eyes filled with tears.

"I'm sorry, too, Cecil," Jessy said with a shiver. "But you're right. You had nothing to do with how I found out what the Klan was going to do. I—I wasn't too smart, I guess. I imagine a lot of people, not just Anna Cora, knew what we were up to."

She had wondered about it for some time, and now she asked, "Cecil, why did you join the Ku Klux Klan?"

He looked at her. "Nobody ever asked me to be in a club before. I wanted to. All the time I was a little kid. They always said,

'No, no, not you, you looney.'" He drew a quick breath and continued, "Then Mr. Hale said I could belong to his club. Help our town be nice, make people be good. I got to wear a sheet like the other fine gentlemen." His shoulders sagged, and he looked at Jessy, bewildered. "Anna Cora says our club is bad. She don't like her father doing things. You know, *visiting* people. She wants me to stop being in the club. Do you think our club is bad, Central?"

"Yes." Jessy sighed. "I'm afraid I do. Cecil, do you understand that it's bad for the Ku Klux Klan to hurt folks who haven't done anything to deserve it?"

"My club does hurt nice people." He nodded. "I don't like that part. But I don't want to get out of my club, the only one I ever got to be in, Central. But if—if we have to hurt any more people," he added sadly, "I'll maybe quit like Anna Cora wants me to."

"I think you will be a lot better off if you do quit the Ku Klux Klan, Cecil. I hope you will. I'm glad we talked tonight."

A few minutes later Jessy saw the handyman to the door. She watched him shuffle down the street, his pockets jingling, loud in the deep, still night. Poor Cecil was going to get hurt, she was afraid. She sighed. But as long as the Klan was around, who was safe?

Hatch came on Saturday night. Once he was with her, Jessy could not let go of him. The fingers of her left hand stayed tightly curled about his arm all through the movie and the long drive they went for afterward in the Moorehouse's Ford.

"Don't think I don't like it, Jessy," he said gently, as he parked the car later by the side of the road, "But if you were a wild grapevine and I was a tree trunk, you'd have me squeezed plumb in two. What's the matter, hon?"

"I'm sorry," Jessy said, embarrassed. But she held onto him still. "I—I'm glad to see you, Hatch. That's all."

"I reckon. But you're scared as hell, too." When she didn't answer him, he said, "Better tell me about it. Ain't takin' you home till you do." He took her hand from his arm and held both of hers tight in his.

Jessy gave in. She told him about Cecil, about the morning glory messages, everything.

Hatch held her close, then sat back with a groan. "I wish we were m—" He hesitated, then went on, "I wish you could come stay with Etta a spell. Could you, Jessy? I want somebody lookin' out for you when I can't."

She thought about it, then shook her head. "I'll be all right in Ardensville. I'm too scared to take many chances, Hatch, believe me. I'm not alone, either. I have friends, good people, as close as my switchboard, a line on the whole community. I could call them in like the cavalry, if I had to, really."

"And me. If ever you need me, Jessy, just call." He kissed her temple. "I'm betwixt in my heart as a blind calf," he told her. "On the one hand, I'm worried stiff something might happen to you. On the other side, I'm right proud that you've been helping them folks. Scared as you are and doin' it anyway."

"I'll be glad it's ended, if it ever is," Jessy confessed honestly.

"For tomorrow at least," he told her, driving back to town, "we can forget this mess and have some fun. There's going to be another rodeo at the Oriel Creek Campgrounds. If your friend Lilli can't come and bring you out, I'll come in to town after you."

"Lilli will bring me, Hatch. She needs a good time, too."

At the telephone office. They stood outside the plate glass door and Hatch held her close a long time. For both of them, Jessy realized, saying good-bye was getting very hard to do.

Chapter 19

"LILLI," JESSY ASKED as they drove toward Oriel Creek and the rodeo, "do you hear from Bill Washburn? Or has he just left you this nice car as a gift?"

"You bet your sweet patootie I hear from him. I got a letter yesterday that made me happier than a duck in a flooded mill pond. Ol' Bill is coming back to Ardensville next month. And guess what, Jessy? He's thinking of getting work in Ardensville and staying around awhile! Little Lilli is counting the days till he comes."

"I'm happy for you, Lilli." Jessy fell silent. Without seeming to, she watched a gray car that was following close behind them. The car had been back there for some time, not once trying to go around them. It could be someone headed for the rodeo as they were, but she didn't recognize the car and couldn't make out the driver.

It was silly to feel that whoever was in the car was keeping an eye on her, but she did.

About an hour later, Lilli parked Bill's roadster among the trees at the campground. The gray car behind purred to a stop beside them. Jessy wasn't surprised when Lombard Hale climbed out. She whispered through a dry throat, "See who I see? He's coming this way!"

Lilli nodded and clasped her hands tight about the steering wheel. "Our good mayor at a country rodeo? Hardly seems the type. But then, neither am I. Don't look like that, Jess. Let's out-bluff him."

Lombard Hale grabbed the roadster's door on the driver's side. He beamed. "Good morning, young ladies. Beautiful day, isn't it?"

Jessy drew a quick breath, half-expecting him to add that it as a "morning glory" day, but he didn't.

As they climbed out, Lombard Hale thumped his chest, inhaled, and said in a kindly good humor, "I love to get out in the country air once in a while, don't you, girls? See, it's brought roses to your cheeks."

Tight-lipped, Jessy mumbled, "Hello." She was desperate to get away, toward the arena, to be near Hatch.

But Lilli hung back and asked the mayor in straight-faced innocence, "Are you riding today, Mr. Hale?"

"No, no, my dear. I'm not." He chuckled. "Riding today! Joking, aren't you, sweetheart?" He saluted them and moved on.

"I'm a real card," Lilli muttered, slamming the car door.

Jessy grabbed Lilli's arm and rushed her toward the gathering crowd. "Another minute near that man, and I'd be sick, Lilli, ever since he caught onto our scheme, and even before that, the night at Joe's, I've been afraid of him."

"Try to forget it for a while," Lilli urged in a soft voice. "We'll both go batty if we don't have some fun now and then."

There wasn't an opportunity right off to talk to Hatch, busy with the rodeo. He waved, though, and Jessy waved back. It was hard to concentrate on the riding and roping going on in front of her. Lombard Hale stood only a few feet from the bench where she sat with Lilli. Hale, well dressed as always, waved a cigar and laughed heartily every few minutes, standing out from the ranchers he spoke to like a peacock from barnyard chickens. He showed little interest in the rodeo events. Was he really here, like he said, just for an outing?

Jessy remembered then that Hale had told her he owned quite a bit of ranchland. Maybe he often picked a day like this to visit with ranching friends. Most ranchers from around were at the rodeo. She had to get it out of her head that he was here because of her. Frowning in deep concentration, Jessy watched a rider bring his bucking bronc to a stylish finish. She clapped furiously.

"It was a pretty good ride," Lilli murmured from the corner of her mouth, "but not that great. Forget Hale. Relax, kid. Nothing's going to happen out here today."

Jessy managed a wobbly grin. "You're right." She wished she could get hold of herself.

"Hatcher Elroy, ridin' Slyfox! Let 'er buck!" Jessy's heart leaped happily at the announcement. The crowd had started to applaud before the announcer's words were finished, reminding her of the high regard these country people had for Hatch.

The sun climbed noon high at last. Jessy went eagerly to meet Hatch striding toward her. They looked at one another for a long moment, no words needed. Jessy was only half aware as Lilli winked, took her sandwiches from their picnic basket, and ambled off with friends from town.

Jessy realized later that they must have eaten, they no doubt talked about the rodeo and other things, but the cowboy's warm smile, his deep blue eyes, could make her forget so much.

"Let's take a walk," he said when they had finished with their food.

Jessy smiled an answer and gathered their things, dropping them into the picnic basket. She wandered along beside him as Hatch carried the basket to Lilli's car parked under a big elm. In another minute, he caught Jessy's hand loosely in his own. She couldn't match his long-legged stride, and he shortened his steps for her. As they walked deeper and deeper into the woods where it was cooler, Hatch turned to smile at her every so often. "You look so beautiful today, Jessy," he told her. "Not as scared as last night. I worried about you all the way back to the ranch."

She admitted, "It's because I'm here with you, Hatch. The more I'm around you, the better I feel." A delighted grin filled his face, and Jessy was glad she had told him how she felt. She smiled when he let go her hand and put his arm about her waist.

After a lengthy silence, Hatch cleared his throat. "I've never met a girl like you before, Jessy. For a long time now I've wanted to tell you—wanted you to know—hell's bells, sweetheart, I *love* you!"

Finally, he'd said it. He loved her! "Oh, Hatch, I love you." They stopped in the path, and Hatch turned her to face him. Jessy trembled as he drew her close. She lifted her face, welcoming his mouth coming down on hers. After a long, delirious moment, Hatch took his lips from hers and smiled lazily into her eyes. His look of love threatened to melt her inside; he kissed her again.

"I love you," Hatch whispered huskily against her hair. "Oh, my darlin' Jessamyn, I love you so much. My lovely, sweet little Jessy."

She snuggled closer. "It feels so good in your arms."

"'Cause that's where you belong." He held her so tight it almost hurt, and then he was letting her go. "We got to start back. I have to finish my fool ridin' this afternoon, honey. But I'm going to be thinkin' about you, about us, ever' minute."

"All—all r-right, Hatch." They walked in step, arms encircling each other's waist, her head resting in the crook of Hatch's shoulder. Jessy felt as though her heart would burst. So this was love, this warm, wonderful feeling that made her heart glad for the very air around her. Pleased with every bird song and every leaf on the trees. Jessy sighed with a contentment she'd never known before in her life.

The soft thud of a footfall in front of them caused Jessy to look ahead. Lombard Hale, smiling, blocked the path. He came forward. "Miss Faber," his tone couldn't have been friendlier, "may I meet your fellow? Who is this good-looking cowboy?" Hale's manicured fingers reached out to shake Hatch's hand.

For a few seconds, Jessy couldn't speak. Then she stammered, "H-Hatch, this is Lombard Hale. Ardensville's mayor. Mr. Hale, this is my friend, Hatcher Elroy." Hatch stiffened beside her at mention of the mayor's name. Jessy looked up at him and was struck by the fury in his eyes.

"I've heard of you. And what I've heard ain't good," Hatch told Hale.

Return hostility flared in the mayor's eyes.

"Don't, Hatch, please," Jessy said. "Let's go."

The mayor smiled and shook his head, surprising Jessy. "I don't know what you've heard, cowboy," he said with a laugh. "It could be somebody has a wrong idea about me. No matter how hard a man tries, he makes a few enemies, you know. People do get mistaken impressions." Both perplexity and good-natured acceptance showed in his look. "Good day, Miss Faber. Mr.—? Elroy, correct?"

"*Hatcher Elroy*. And make no mistake about it: if any harm comes to this girl, *my girl*, the gent responsible will have to account to me, Mr. Mayor, sir."

Lombard Hale looked crushed. "Now, now," he chuckled, "don't get huffy, cowboy. I really can't think what has you folks acting so unfriendly on such a beautiful day. Why would I, or anyone else for that matter, want to hurt pretty Jessy Faber?" An odd look came into his eyes, not fear or anger or anything else Jessy could name. But a—sickness, a kind of disturbance, seemed to reflect from deep inside him.

She looked quickly away and hoped it was only her imagination.

Hatch maneuvered them around Hale and told him in a cold voice, "I figure this matter settled, Hale. I meant what I said."

The man shrugged without comment and followed several paces behind them as Jessy and Hatch walked back to the rodeo. Later, with immense relief, Jessy watched Hale get into his car and drive off in the direction of Ardensville. Hatch, and nothing else, was going to have her full attention the rest of the afternoon.

She sat with Lilli and watched Hatch tie an enormous red steer's legs out in the arena. Lilli said, "Your face makes me think of a—a May sunrise, or something."

Jessy sighed and turned to look at Lilli. "Lilli, he loves me. Hatch told me so, today. And—and I love him, so much." Her voice shook as she went on, "I keep thinking what a miracle it is, my coming to Ardensville. I wouldn't have met him, otherwise."

Later, Jessy looked at Hatch, riding as pickup man for another rider. "See him out there? So rugged and strong and at the same time, Lilli, he's gentle and kind."

"Hoooeee," Lilli teased, "and you left out that he's handsomer than the dickens."

"Oh, that, too," Jessy agreed with a breathless laugh. "He is good-looking. But Hatch is a lot more. I'm lucky, Lilli. And I'm not sure I deserve it. I can hardly believe this is happening to me."

"You do like him a trifle, don't you?" Lilli continued to tease her.

Jessy struggled to find just the right words, "Lilli," she said finally, "Hatch has my heart, totally."

"Hmm," Lilli exclaimed, "Maybe I can use that in a story—"

"Lilli!" Jessy protested, frowning.

"Just joking, kid. I hate missing this stuff," she told her, "but it's time I moved our car into the shade again. Sun's moved around. If I don't repark it, it will be like getting into an oven when we're ready to go home."

"Run off, see if I care." Jessy pretended to be miffed. "Making fun of me!"

Lilli gave a hearty laugh. "I'll be back in a few minutes. You can tell me more. I won't be mean."

"Good." When Lilli was gone, Jessy turned her attention to Hatch, out in the arena.

Lilli was gone for about ten minutes. Longer than it should have taken to move the car. Jessy began to watch for her return, wondering. And when finally she spotted Lilli coming out of the trees, it looked as if Lilli were having trouble. She zigzagged from side to side in the path. A chill chased along Jessy's spine.

Then as Lilli neared, Jessy could see that her face was chalk white and her eyes stared wildly. "*Lilli!*" Jessy jumped to her feet and ran to her. Lilli spewed forth a jumble of words that made no sense. And before Jessy could catch her, she stumbled, made a slow turn with blank eyes looking skyward, then dropped to the dusty ground in a faint.

"Help!" Jessy screamed. "Bring water, somebody, please!" She kneeled and drew Lilli's head into her lap. "Oh, Lilli, what's happened? What's wrong?" With trembling fingers, she smoothed the silvery-blonde tendrils back from Lilli's face. "Lilli, wake up. Please."

Jessy looked frantically toward the arena. The show had stopped. Someone must have passed the word about Lilli's fainting. And had heard her own cry for help. Audience and performers alike were running toward them. When they crowded in on her, Jessy begged, "Please stand back. My friend needs air. I don't know what's wrong. Has anyone seen Hatcher Elroy? I need him."

"Is the lady dead?" A small child pushed against Jessy's shoulder to ask solemnly.

Jessy shook her head. "The lady is fine. She'll be all right, I think. Go find your mother, honey, please." In a moment a hand shoved a cup of water to Jessy. She put it on the ground and soaked her hanky in it, then bathed Lilli's face. "Wake up, Lilli. Tell me what's wrong? It's Jessy, Lilli, Jessy. Talk to me."

It seemed like an eternity, then Lilli's pale lashes fluttered. "Lilli!" Jessy cried, "come on, come out of it, Lilli." In another second the hazel eyes stared up at Jessy and began to fill with tears.

"Ohh," Lilli moaned, stirring in Jessy's arms. "I can't stand it—didn't want to look—oh, no-oo."

"What, Lilli? What?" Jessy was instantly thankful when Hatch came to a halt on a knee beside her. "I don't know what happened," she told him. "Lilli went to move our car into a shadier place and she—she came back like this," Jessy finished on a choking sob.

"Take it easy, honey," Hatch said. "Give her a minute to come around. She's had a shock, I reckon. Take it easy, Jessy," he soothed.

Tenderly, Jessy wiped Lilli's face again, and suddenly, Lilli tried to sit up. Jessy helped, feeling swift relief. "You're all right. Everything's fine, Lilli."

Sudden dry sobs wrenched Lilli's whole body. Jessy put her face against Lilli's and held her tight. "What is it, Lilli, what's wrong?" She shook Lilli, gently.

It seemed to help. Lilli's sobs ebbed after a moment. She looked first to Jessy, then at Hatch. "A gr-grave," she whispered brokenly. "Somebody in it."

"A *grave*?" Jessy choked. "What grave, Lilli, what are you trying to tell us?"

"My—my car," Lilli cried brokenly, struggling to sit up straighter. "I was m-moving the roadster around to the other side, a woodsier place. Shade. Cooler. My rear tire—" An expression of pure horror came to Lilli's face as she seemed to remember something. For a few seconds she sobbed harshly, then went on. "My rear tire sa-sank—in a hole. I went to see. Saw him. A man, a b-body in a grave. Under my t-tire."

Jessy's hands dropped. She sat back, feeling numb all over. But Lilli wasn't finished. "I screamed. A man heard me, and he came and l-looked, too. He said—he said, from the clothes, the sh-shoes, it was the dancing Greek, dead. Jessy"—her eyes filled with fresh tears—"Julio Salonika is dead. He's in the grave."

Jessy's heart constricted. "Are you all right, honey?" Hatch asked, squeezing her shoulder. She nodded, and he asked, "Can you stay with Lilli? I'll go see what this is all about." Hatch hurriedly joined the crowd that thronged toward the opposite side of the grove. "Wait," he called, "some of you might not want to see—"

Jessy got Lilli to a bench, and the two sat stiffly. Around a fist pressed to her mouth, Lilli mumbled over and over, "The poor children. Those poor Salonika babies. Their *uncle*."

Hatch came back. "The man in the grave was shot, murder," he told Jessy quietly; his hands covered hers on Lilli's arm. "Several people from Ardensville say the same thing—that he is—was, a dancing man who spent a few months in town last winter. There's talk the Ku Klux Klan did this."

She nodded, her eyes on Hatch's face. "I knew him," she said in a whisper. "Hatch, it was me who had Julio Salonika come to Ardensville. He wouldn't have come, except for me. He would be alive. This is my fault," she said, "this is my fault, *again*—"

Hatch stared at her. "No," he insisted, "this isn't your doing, Jessy. Stop talking like this. You couldn't hurt anyone, honey." He drew her up, and then he took Lilli's arm and helped her to her feet at the same time. "I'm takin' you girls home."

Jessy stared at him. "Farley, first," she whimpered. Saying it aloud didn't ease the awfulness inside her. "Now Julio. My fault. I made them both—die." She held herself stiffly upright, putting one foot in front of the other as she walked alongside Hatch. He tried to put an arm around her, and Jessy resisted. "Not you," she said, looking up at him through a blur. "I won't let it happen to you, too."

She would go away, far away. She didn't say it aloud, knowing instinctively that Hatch would try to stop her. But she had to get out of his life before something happened to him.

Catching sight of her face, Hatch grabbed Jessy and pulled her against him. "You're in shock, honey. Because you knew the guy, it's hard on you, too. But you'll get over it." He crooned in her ear, "You just need rest, darlin'." He motioned to a cowboy friend passing them. "Hey, help this lady, here." He pointed to Lilli, waiting, stone-still. Hatch picked Jessy up and cuddled her tight, subduing her struggles as he carried her the rest of the way to Lilli's roadster.

If she couldn't convince him she was all right, Jessy realized dimly, Hatch wouldn't let her out of his sight. Yet she had to be left alone, so she could leave. A few miles from Ardensville, she managed to say, "I'm sorry, Hatch, for acting up back there. I went a little crazy for a minute or two. I'm fine now."

He sighed and kissed her forehead. Tears filled Jessy's eyes. Death followed her. From Seena to Ardensville. Hatch, the person she loved most of all, must live. She was wrong to have thought her troubles were over and that she could be happy here. She had to go, go far!

At her door, Hatch held her so tightly Jessy had difficulty breathing. "I'll be all right," she said for the twentieth time.

"How can I leave you here alone?" he whispered as if to himself. "How can I go back to the ranch and work? I want to look out for you."

Jessy thought quickly. "But I'm not in danger," she protested in as bright a voice as she could muster. "Since this—this murder has been found out, the county sheriff will be here. He'll be digging into Ardensville's troubles, now. There'll be a stop to the Klan and everything bad." She said softly, "It's over, Hatch, all over. Truly, I feel better."

For a long moment he said nothing. "I reckon you're right," he agreed finally. "But I sure as hell ain't happy about leaving you here, anyway."

"Hatch, you're being silly. I'll be all right!"

All night Jessy tossed, sleepless. In the morning she rang Gussie Stuberg. "I'm giving notice, Mrs. Stuberg. I have to quit my job. I can only stay on a few days—give you time to find some-one to take my place."

"What are you talkin' about?" Gussie's sleepy voice rose to a shout. "You can't quit, Jessy!"

"I'm sorry. Two weeks is the absolute longest I can stay. I have to get off the line, Mrs. Stuberg. There are other calls to take care of." Jessy's hand trembled violently as she closed the key and pulled out the cords. It was good-bye to Ardensville, to everyone, to—*Hatch*. A terrible pain twisted inside her.

Chapter 20

AFTER THE DISCOVERY of the body at Oriel Creek Campground, telephone subscribers clamored to one another over the shock they felt; a murder had never happened this close to Ardensville! Each time she overheard the gossip, Jessy realized the horror of it herself.

Such a thing would never happen again and be her fault. She would go to Chicago. Or Minneapolis, or New York, and lose herself. If only Gussie would stop dragging her feet. She was making little effort to find someone to take her place. But if Gussie didn't hurry, she'd have to work the switchboard singlehanded.

Hatch came to see Jessy several times. Each time it was nearly midnight, after his sixteen-hour workday on the ranch. She begged him not to worry about her and hid her true feelings, her true intentions. And when he called one day to say that he and Tom Moorehouse had to make an important trip to the Kansas City stockyards and would be gone a week, Jessy sent up a small tearful prayer of thanks.

A uniformed county sheriff accompanied by two investigators wearing dull-colored baggy suits and carrying notebooks had come to Ardensville the morning following the finding of Julio Salonika's body.

Eventually they came to the telephone office to question Jessy, as she'd known they would. From time to time, between calls as she worked at the switchboard, the policemen questioned her. Jessy told them all she knew about Julio Salonika, from the time she had called him in New York up to the day of his disappearance.

"That's all?" the shorter investigator pried. His shrewd glance dug at her deepest thoughts. "Tell me, Miss Faber, you got an idea who did this?"

"Everybody in town has an idea who killed Julio Salonika." She gave him a direct answer, although she felt sick at the pit of her stomach. "The Ku Klux Klan. Julio Salonika was Greek. A foreigner. The Klan has been making trouble for people like Julio for months, trying to drive them out of Ardensville. Especially Lombard Hale." She might be able to get out of town before Lombard Hale and the rest of the Klan found out she had openly accused them. Maybe not. It didn't seem to matter.

She told about Hale being out at the rodeo, the same day Julio was found. "Maybe he was checking on the grave. Making sure it hadn't been found. I understand the—the body had been there a long time, months.

"I've made a list of people you should talk to," she told the sheriff. "Some positive Klan members, others I'm guessing at." The list lay ready on the board in front of her. Jessy rubbed her palms together to dry them, picked up the paper, and handed it to the county sheriff. Lombard Hale's name topped the list, followed by others. If only they could be rounded up, before they could come for her…. She'd left Cecil Kinglake off the list. She hoped that wasn't wrong. In his own way, the handyman would always be innocent.

After a few more questions, requests for addresses, and directions for finding various homes, the investigators left.

Watching them go, Jessy felt a queer mixture of satisfaction and fear. She'd done what she could. Julio Salonika's killer, or killers, would be found out and brought to trial. Although it wouldn't bring poor Julio back, she was glad she'd had courage enough to tell the sheriff who might be responsible. She'd done so little of worth in her life. Only damage.

She could not, Jessy realized, leave without seeing Lilli one more time, to tell her good-bye. She found Lilli hidden away in the beautiful old house, pale, listless, with little to say. The dismal visit left Jessy feeling more tormented than ever. Bill Washburn, who had arrived back in Ardensville two days before, saw her to the door.

"Lilli has rough nightmares," he told Jessy with a frown. "She keeps finding that body, that grave, over and over again. Lilli's always behaved like a strong, outgoing person, but she's soft inside. This is too tough for her to handle."

"Will she be all right?" Jessy winked back the tears.

"I've had the doctor in three or four times to see her. He says it might take a long time for her to recover, or—she could snap out of it tomorrow. The mind, the emotions, are hard to second-guess."

Jessy nodded that she understood. "If there's anything I can do, Mr. Washburn—Bill—before I go, please let me know. You'll take care of her?"

"Absolutely. When she comes out of this and feels better, I'm going to ask Lilli to marry me." His face flushed. "Whether her answer is yes or no, I plan to stay on in Ardensville. All the time I was on the road, I kept remembering the Christmas Pageant we went to. The Klan. Those little kids." He shook his head and slammed the heel of his palm against the doorjamb. "I could kick myself for not doing something then, standing up for what I believe. Anyhow, I'm here, ready to do my part to rid this pretty town of the *rot* that's ruining it."

"I'm glad," Jessy told him. Maybe Bill Washburn could do something about the Klan. She and Lilli hadn't gotten far. Whether Bill did, or not, she'd never know because she wouldn't be here. "If I don't see Lilli again, tell her for me that I'll always think of her as my dearest friend. Always, wherever I am.

❂

"I DON'T BLAME YOU a bit for leaving." Lucian spat bitterly when Jessy visited to tell the Salonikas good-bye. "The Ku Klux Klan has won. They will never go now." His dark eyes were somber, deeply angry. "If I didn't go to the store for food, Grandmother and the kids would starve. They're so scared they'll be seen and hurt, I can't get them to leave the house."

"It's awful," Jessy whispered. "Awful." She reached out to touch him, but Lucian jerked away.

"Everybody knows it was the Klan that had Uncle Julio killed. Because he was *foreign trash*, like Grandma and me. Hale wanted to get rid of us, and him, and others. Julio must have fought back, though it's hard to picture."

The boy looked so distressed, Jessy begged, "Lucian, stop. Don't talk about it anymore."

He glared and went on, "The Klan probably intended to kill Mr. Burmann, but he got away from them th just a bad beating. He was right to take the first train out of town. Did you know the McGuires are gone?"

"I didn't know." Jessy pictured the big Irish family, once so happy. "No, Lucian, I didn't know."

"Whole family left in the middle of the night, right after they heard Uncle Julio was found murdered. Left their house, furniture, everything. Took only their clothes. Just disappeared. It isn't fair!"

There was nothing she could do. "You're right, Luc, it isn't fair. Maybe—you and the children and Grandma should go, too."

He shook his head. The ugliness of his expression softened.

"First time I laid eyes on this town, I thought it was the most beautiful place on earth. It was so much like the town Mama and Papa always talked of finding; a place for them, a nice place to bring up their family in." His voice caught; Lucian shook his head. Anger flashed once more in his eyes as he told Jessy, "I wanted to see the police find and punish the ones who killed Uncle Julio. But nobody cares, not really, and everyone's scared."

When he saw Jessy about to argue, he insisted, "I can tell when I'm around town. Nobody's going to mind very much if they don't find the killer. Uncle Julio was human garbage after all, not much account to anybody in town."

"That's enough, Lucian! Enough. It isn't true; they *will* find his killer, they will."

"Save your breath, *Central*. You feel the same way I do, I can see it in your face. You're leaving, remember? You'd stay if you felt different."

How could she argue with that? Jessy hugged the Salonikas one by one. She left the little house with the feeling that she'd come to town, stirred up a hornets nest, and was now turning away before seeing if anyone recovered from the stings. It couldn't be any other way, though.

The investigation into Julio's death, after the first flurry, slowed. Lucian insisted the law officials were bought off by the Klan. Jessy chose to believe that they couldn't find enough good evidence to confirm Julio's killer. According to a report in the *Ardensville Times*, the case was not closed, but the reporter hinted that Julio's death might go unsolved if someone didn't come forward with new evidence.

What had happened? Jessy wondered. She had no way of knowing how it had come about that Julio was killed, or where. Like Farley's death, though, Julio's would be forever on her conscience.

At work, Jessy decided she could say good-bye to others in the community by way of a public announcement. The Klan would be glad to see her go. Hatch, out of town, wouldn't hear about it or try to stop her.

She wanted to thank the many good people she'd served the past year. The Bakers, who never knew what time it was unless they asked her. Old Hannah Lewelling who called her sister, Marvella, every night at the stroke of seven, to talk. Mrs. Jordan, always wanting Central to check up on her husband and make sure he wasn't loitering on the street when she'd sent him into town for groceries. So many more.

Squaring her shoulders, taking a deep breath, Jessy rang six longs. "This is Central speaking. I have a personal message. I'm leaving Ardensville for good. B-before I go, I'd like to tell those of you who have been my f-friends—made my stay here...." Jessy's voice broke. She couldn't talk anymore. She closed the keys and pulled down the cords. Within seconds, flaps began to drop. Jessy turned her back to them. She put her face in her hands and wept.

In a short while, the telephone office door burst open. "Get them calls!" Gussie Stuberg shouted, puffing to where Jessy sat crying. "Had to run all the way down here to see what in thunder's going on. Tried to call you and talk some sense into your pretty little noodle, and you wouldn't answer. Me, your boss! Your job here ain't finished yet. Get them calls, miss!"

Through her tears, Jessy saw that Gussie meant what she said. Wiping her face with the backs of her hands, she drew a long breath and turned to face the switchboard. There was scarcely a flap that wasn't down. She took up a plug and pushed it into a brass-rimmed hole. "N-number, pl-please? she whispered.

"Please, Central, *don't go.*" It wasn't what Jessy expected to hear. Mrs. Johnson pleaded over the line, "Please, you can't leave us. What would we do without you? Central, I always called you first in an emergency. I prayed to God, second. Don't go."

Jessy couldn't reply. When Mrs. Johnson's phone clicked, she pulled the plugs and took another call.

"Do you got to go, Central?" It was young Mrs. Harmon, who lived on the south end of town across the tracks. "I wisht you wouldn't. You saved my baby's life last winter, Central. Remember when the blizzard got so bad? My baby was dyin' of pneumonia, but you got the doc here in time."

What were these people telling her? Jessy turned her tear-stained face to look at her boss. Gussie Stuberg grinned from ear to ear. Her voice was gentle, "I got a good idea what you're hearin' from them calls. Don't sit idle, girl. I see at least forty more flaps, waitin'. I'd help, but them calls will all be for you."

Jessy smiled. A knot of ill-feeling about herself that had been inside her for a very long time began to crumble. Through a film she faced the board, lifted a plug, and one by one, she took the calls.

"You got the fire department out to our place in time. Saved our whole summer hay crop stored in that burnin' barn. Thanks a lot, Central."

"I won a blue ribbon for the gooseberry jam recipe that was your mama's, Central. You give it to me when I asked, last August fair time."

"I passed my spelling test," a youngster's voice piped, "'cause you made me spell 'retaliation' back to you *five times*, Central. I was mad at you then, but I sure was happy when I passed."

If she listened to any more calls, she would be a blubbering pile of jelly. Jessy whirled and buried her face against Mrs. Stuberg's waiting shoulder. "I don't want to go," she said, her voice muffled. "I don't *want* to go to Chicago, or back to The Ranch, or anywhere else. I want to stay here. But I can't."

"Now, Central, you heard them folks," Gussie soothed. "They can't get along without you." She stroked Jessy's back like she might a baby's. "There, there. I'll take over for you at the board, for a while. You go on back to your room and try to pull yourself together. Think it over good. This town needs you, honey."

Jessy stumbled blindly toward the back room. For the next ten minutes, she lay on the cot, her mind an aching whirl of confused thought. She wanted to stay. But as long as Lombard Hale ruled the town, there would be trouble. She'd turned his name over to the police, on top of everything else. Hale would be after her. Hatch would step in, and he might be hurt—*killed*.

The first morning train went east. Jessy stood up and started to pack in a hurry. She would try to get some sleep and be out of here at dawn.

A while later, around eight o'clock, she heard Gussie Stuberg leave to go home for the night. The telephone office was quiet. Too quiet. Jessy tossed all night, her constant movement disturbing Cowboy at the foot of her bed. He meowed to be let out.

It seemed that dawn would never come. A freak summer storm commenced about daylight, putting an end to Jessy's last chance for an hour or two of sleep. Aching and tired in every limb, she got up, washed, and put on her navy and white traveling dress.

This was the day, the end of her life in Ardensville, the end of any life she and Hatch might have had together. Jessy put her nightgown and toiletries in her already-packed satchel. There was nothing to do now, except call Augusta Stuberg and tell her she was leaving right away, not waiting. Someone else would have to carry on today, taking the town's calls. It would not be Jessy Faber.

Oddly, Gussie Stuberg didn't argue when Jessy called. A short while later, Jessy looked around the back room to be sure she hadn't forgotten anything, satchel in hand. The main door opened from the outside, and Gussie Stuberg blew in, bedraggled from the storm. She grinned, her step was unsteady.

Not again! Not today! "I'm not staying another minute," Jessy told her. "You've been drinking again, but you'll have to take care of the board, anyway. I don't care what happens!" She started around her weaving boss.

Gussie waggled her fingers. "Bye-bye."

Jessy wondered fleetingly if Gussie Stuberg was pulling this stunt to keep her here. No, she reasoned, even Gussie wouldn't stoop to such a silly extreme. "I thought you'd stopped drinking, Mrs. Stuberg," she turned to say. "I thought you and Mr. Munker had an understanding, that you were truly happy?"

"Ol' soul is 'hout of town," Gussie told her. She blinked and began to drag herself out of her rain-soaked coat.

Jessy's shoulders sagged. She would be out of town herself in less than half an hour, headed east. Unless—she waited for the later, westbound train. Would a few hours make a difference? It made none to her which way she went, as far as trains were concerned.

She opened her mouth to speak when a clap of thunder seemed to shake the telephone office. Gussie jumped and cowered like a scared child.

With a sigh, Jessy put the satchel down. Mrs. Stuberg was in no condition to handle things if a serious emergency call came through the switchboard. There could be several emergencies if this storm held on. Lightning could cause fires. "Go to my room—go to the back room," Jessy corrected herself, "and lie down. As soon as I can, I'll get you some coffee from Mandy's. You're a mess, Mrs. Stuberg," she said bluntly.

"I—ah, come to work!" Gussie hiccuped. "C-come to work." She stared, reminding Jessy of a homely, blinking, huge baby bird.

"You can hardly stand up, let alone handle the switchboard. C'mon. You're going back to bed." Gussie leaned so heavily against Jessy that both of them tripped twice and nearly fell before they reached the back room.

Chapter 21

THUNDER RUMBLED and crashed outside. Jessy went to the switchboard. For the moment, she could be glad Gussie kept her here. It would be scary out there on the street, walking to the depot, waiting for the train.

The storm raged on, darkening the room. Jessy took a minute to turn on the overhead lightbulb. With a feeling of frantic helplessness, she watched the switchboard go crazy—electricity in the air caused the metal flaps to drop every-which-where. Time after time, Jessy plugged in to find silence, not a real call. And there was no way to tell if a subscriber was trying to call in, or if the drop was storm-caused, unless she tried them. Jessy began to perspire. Thankfully, the few real calls she caught were not emergencies, yet.

An hour later, Jessy looked up in surprise as Cecil Kinglake came through the door, his pockets jangling. He carried his toolbox. "You must know the whole switchboard is a mess when there's an electrical storm," she told him, waving at the clicking drops. "But there isn't anything you can do, Cecil. It's the storm. Mrs. Stuberg and I have talked about this before."

Instead of turning to leave, Cecil came shuffling on toward her. "It's a wire in back I come to see to," he told her, "one other time I was here, I saw it was wearing thin, about in two. Needs splicing."

"Wait until the storm is over," Jessy said. "You can't tell a thing about this switchboard with the storm carrying on. And—and you might get an electrical shock." Was Cecil crying? Jessy wondered suddenly, studying him. He saw her watching and he looked away, wiping his eyes with a balled fist. He went around to the backside of the switchboard, so slow his shoe soles might have been caught in a quagmire.

She felt edgy, a kind of warning nudged at the back of her mind. "What on earth is the matter!" she cried. All at once, the warning exploded—*they* were trying to kill her! Jessy flew off the stool and backed swiftly away from the switchboard. Cecil, out of sight, was making noises, and before her staring eyes the switchboard loomed—a monster, black death.

"Cecil, stop!" Jessy shrieked. "Do you plan to fix wires so I will be—electrocuted? Stop it! Who sent you to do this? Lombard Hale? The Klan?" She shivered violently.

A soft choking sob from in back of the switchboard brought a clearness to Jessy's mind. "Cecil, come here, please." An eternity passed. Then Cecil shuffled out, his pockets noisy, a pair of pliers in his hand. "Cecil," Jessy said, "let's talk about this. Come talk to me, please, What did you come here for today, be honest?"

He wagged his head. "I can't tell you. If I tell, Mr. Hale won't ever let me see Anna Cora again. He said, *never*, I—I couldn't stand not seeing my Annie," he whispered.

"I understand." Jessy said, trying to think. In a moment, she said, "Cecil, if I guess why you came, it won't be your fault that I know. I think the mayor has wanted to be rid of me, maybe for some time. Then, the storm that started in the night gave him an idea for—doing away with me. If I was electrocuted, because of a short in the wires or something, the storm could be blamed. Isn't that it? Mr. Hale would be innocent, and so would you." The look on Cecil's face, his harsh sobs, told her it was the truth. "I was going to leave today," she choked out through a dry throat. "I would have thought that would have been enough."

Cecil shook his head. "Mr. Hale didn't think you'd really go. He says you'll make more trouble for our Klan club and—" Cecil looked further distressed. "I wasn't supposed to tell anything. Now me and Anna Cora—"

"It will be all right. We'll think of something," Jessy told him quickly, to reassure him, though she knew there was really little they could do. She caught his hand in hers.

"I—I can't hurt you, Central," he said, giving her a big hug. "You're my friend. I can't kill people, anyway. Mr. Hale shouldn't ask me to."

"Just a second, Cecil," Jessy said, her blood running icy cold, "I want to ask you something else. Do you know what happened, what really happened, to Julio Salonika, the dancing man?"

Now that he'd opened up, Cecil seemed eager to talk. "I didn't want to bury the dancing man in the woods at Oriel Creek. Mr. Hale made me do it. Like what he wanted me to do to you, he said if I don't do what he says, I don't get to see Annie."

The storm outside seemed to be letting up. Jessy remembered the switchboard, that calls needed to be taken care of even while this strange scene was taking place inside the telephone office. Surprised that she could be this calm, she climbed back on the stool and from time to time took the calls.

"You didn't kill Julio yourself, then?" she asked Cecil.

"I wouldn't do that!" he exclaimed. He looked insulted. "I told you, Central, I can't kill nobody."

"I'm sorry I had to ask you. But do you know what happened?"

"I wasn't there when he was killed. It was later, Mr. Hale made me come get the dancing man, all bloody and dead, from his auto store. Mr. Hale said the dancing man was a—a *bolshevik*, a trouble-maker, that he hated America. Mr. Hale said he killed the danc-ing man because he had to."

Jessy told Cecil, whitefaced, "Julio Salonika wouldn't have hurt anyone. Mr. Hale is lying. He didn't even know Julio well." Beginning to get a glimmer of an idea, a way to end all this for good, she asked. "Do you know about other things that hap-pened? Bad things to hurt people?"

"We started fires," Cecil mumbled, "and we threw rocks, and—"

His head jerked, and he stopped speaking when a flying figure passed by outside the plate glass window of the telephone office. The door was yanked open. "Annie?" Cecil questioned, starting toward her, "are you all right?"

Anna Cora was plainly relieved to see Cecil. Her glance darted from his face to Jessy's and back to him. "I—I ran away. From Papa. He means to hurt *you*. I told him he mustn't hurt anybody anymore. He has to stop that. We have to make him stop. He scared me—Daddy came—at *me*. I ran to find you, Cecil."

It numbed Jessy to think that Hale was threatening his own child. There was a change in Cecil's manner, his voice came strong. "I'm here, Anna Cora. I'm right here."

She needed witnesses to all this, Jessy realized. Not just one or two. Hundreds. She needed to reach out to every decent, thinking person with what Cecil and Anna Cora had told her. The two of them were innocents; she hated to involve them, but they alone could tell the truth. As for herself, she had the best reason in the world to do this. Since coming to Ardensville she'd gained so much—dear friends, Lilli, the Salonikas, Hatch, others. For too long she had been afraid, holding back. It was her turn to give something to all of them, now.

There was no magic eraser to undo the past, but here and

now—in the present—she could do something about the future. Would the mayor's followers continue to join him if they could hear the whole truth, all at once? With care, Jessy explained to Anna Cora and Cecil: "If we tell people the truth about the bad things that have happened here in Ardensville, I think we can stop the Klan from ever hurting anyone else again.

"We can make a public announcement through my switchboard. We will tell the entire town, everyone who can hear us, about the murder of Julio Salonika and the other Klan wrongs. Everyone will know for themselves, then, what the Klan really is."

They looked at her wonderingly. "Do you want to do this?" she asked gently. "The two of you will be doing most of the talking." She looked into Anna Cora's concerned eyes. "What we're about to do will make your father angry, do you understand? He will probably go to jail, too." Turning to Cecil, she said, "Until he's taken, the three of us may be in danger. You know that, don't you? If you are against my idea—"

"I want Papa to stop hurting people," Anna Cora answered her. "My grandpa and grandma are dead now, but they wouldn't like what Papa's doing to their beautiful town. Papa is *sick*. He needs help, I think."

"Annie and me will tell," Cecil decided. "We'll help. This is a good thing; I want to do it."

Jessy nodded and managed a steady smile. "It's settled, then. Here we go, before we lose our nerve." She rang six longs for a public announcement. Her voice quivered with emotion as she spoke into the mouthpiece, "This is Jessamyn Faber, Central, making a plea for help. Everyone within hearing of my voice, please, please, think about this: The Ku Klux Klan is a—a blight that has diseased this town. It is bad enough"—her voice firmed— "that in the past year Ardensville has become a—a mire of suspicion and hate. And fear. Honest businessmen forced to close their stores and leave town. People, right in their own homes, tormented and hurt. Now there has been a murder. A *murder*. Shall we let this go on, and on? Many of you have agreed with the Klan, evidently seeing Klan aims as right and good. But I have two people here with me at the telephone exchange who can tell you differently. More than most of us, they know the truth about the Klan. Listen to what they say. The first who will speak to you, Cecil Kinglake, is an ex-Klan member." With a thumping heart, Jessy put the headset on Cecil and adjusted the mouthpiece. He looked at her, and Jessy nodded for him to go ahead.

He faltered at first, yet his voice was deadly earnest. "I am Cecil K-Kinglake. I—I want to tell you about the bad things I have done—because I wanted so much to belong to the Klan club. I was there was the little children in the woods' shack was set afire. Mr. Lombard Hale told me to throw the match. Those kids weren't hurting anybody. They shouldn't be hurt, either. Mr. Pierce at the drugstore, and me, and some others, took the McGuire babies away from their yard and we hid them 'way upstairs in Mr. Hale's house—to scare their mama and daddy so they wouldn't want to live in Ardensville no more.

"We made Mrs. McGuire so sad, so scared." He said after a hesitation, "I didn't like that. I was with the Klan club, wearing our sheets, when we did the other fires and threw rocks in the night to scare people. I didn't beat up Mr. Burmann, but I know who did. I will tell the police. I didn't kill the dancing man, either," Cecil said quickly. "Mr. Hale made me come and get him out of a brand new car. Mr. Hale was so mad because the dancing man bled all over in the car. He died there. Mr. Hale made me take the dancing man's body to the Oriel Creek Campground and bury it there. He said nobody'd find it. But if they did, they would think the bones was some stranger, a traveler who got sick and died and his people just put him under the ground.

"None of the things our Klan club did was nice. The Klan should not do bad things anymore. Now, my sweetheart, Anna Cora Hale, would like to talk to you." Cecil took off the headpiece and put it on Anna Cora. He gave her a soft, encouraging smile.

"This is Anna Cora. You know me. You know my father. Everything Cecil told you is true. My papa did these things. I think he is sick. People who are well should not let him do bad things. Don't be mean to him, don't hurt my papa, but don't help him do these wrong things anymore." Anna Cora began to cry. "I don't love Papa when he's bad." Cecil put an arm around her shoulder and rocked Annie back and forth.

A sound from the back of the room made the three of them turn. "You mean Lombard Hale is the head of the Klan, he's behind these terrible things?" Augusta Stuberg stood there, looking upset, yet more sober than Jessy had ever seen her.

"Mrs. Stuberg! You did trick me. But you looked so—"

"Drunk? Nearly ruined this dress, dousing it with firewater so I'd smell like a drunk. Did my act as good as Mary Pickford could've, didn't I? I knew it would keep you here. You got a giant conscience, sweetie."

Jessy waved her hands wildly. "Yes, I'm still here, but the world could crack over my head in the next minute, Mrs. Stuberg. If you've been listening to us, you know we're in trouble. Will you please get Anna Cora and Cecil out of here? Hide them. Take them—take them to Lilli. Bill Washburn's there, and he'll help us."

"You come, too, honey," Gussie insisted. "If Lombard did the things you three claim, you could get hurt."

"I'll come," Jessy promised. "Go now, hurry. I'm going to call Lilli's to tell them we're on our way. Bill Washburn can be on the lookout for us. Then I'm going to call the county sheriff at Macloud and tell him to get here as fast as he can. I'll be right behind you."

Jessy quickly completed the calls and turned to leave. On the eleven line a flap dropped. She hesitated. Alice Harmon's second baby was past due. She could be in a bad way, need the doctor. Jessy plugged into the eleven line. "Alice, what number?"

"Central, I'm callin' to thank you. My husband, Boone, went to his first Ku Klux Klan meetin' the other night. He ain't goin' to no more. Thanks for tellin' us all how that bunch really does their dirty work. I want to bring up my babies in a town that's clean and good. But we don't need the Klan."

"Fine. You're welcome. Alice, if you don't need anything else, I'd better get off the line. Good-bye."

She hesitated a few second longer as other drops clicked down on the board. No, she couldn't take the chance, she'd better go. Jessy slipped off the stool and ran for the door. The doorknob turned roughly in her hand. The door slammed into her, knocking her backward. He had been there on the other side of the glass door. In her hurry she hadn't seen him. Lombard Hale. He pushed his way inside.

Chapter 22

THE MAYOR'S FACE WAS beaded with perspiration, his eyes were glassy. "You condemned me, Miss Faber!" he roared, shoving her hard in the direction of the switchboard. "Now, my people—my town, will hear me." He pushed her again. "Get over there, work that thing for a public announcement. It is my turn to tell the people my side." Frozen with fear, Jessy couldn't move. Hale twisted her arm. "Show me what to do, Miss Central!"

Like a trembling, mindless robot, Jessy finally was able to set her body in motion. She pointed a shaking finger at the stool; the mayor sat down, his shoulders back, his expression wildly belligerent. She placed the headset on his head and her shaking fingers tangled for a second in his hair, causing her to yank her hand back as if it had been burned.

She rang to signal a public announcement, then whirled to run, but Hale caught her wrist in an iron grip. Jessy's head buzzed, her entire being was gripped in a feeling of terror, but she heard the mayor begin:

"This is Lombard Arden Hale, your mayor, speaking. You've heard charges brought against me. Terrible things have been said, but I can explain. It isn't me who has brought harm to Ardensville. It is *them*. I love this town. I've always wanted only what's best for it. Named for my people," he mumbled, "meant to be clean, a beautiful city. No room for Jews, Negroes, Catholics, for aliens who force their dark faces and strange ways into my town. If you are for the white race, people, then it only follows that you are against the others. It must be that way. If we love and care about our heritage, our main concern, no matter what, must be one-hundred percent Americanism!"

Incoherent at times, Hale went on, "—protect, keep clean and decent—all I ever want to do for you." He sounded close to sobbing. "A little rough stuff has been necessary, you understand. I didn't kill that black Greek. He came to me to talk about opening a *dance studio*, and I told him, 'You won't dance in my town!' I ordered him to leave Ardensville. He said he would not. I showed the bolshevik troublemaker my gun; to show he'd go, or else. Fired into his leg, he was bleeding all over my store, must have hit an artery. I didn't kill him. If he wanted help, I said, he could crawl for it. He got into one of my *new cars*, bled to death...."

Jessy twisted her numb wrist inside his hand. If he was finished with his speech, she was next. His grip held. He smiled suddenly at the board. "I want all you people who agree with me to call me back. I know you will agree with me that we must carry on, we must unite forever and stand tall for a white America, a pure city!"

Lombard Hale kept his eyes intent on the board. For one of the few times Jessy could remember, nowhere on it did a flap drop. Hale frowned. He turned his glazed expression on her. "Something is wrong!" He shouted. "This switchboard isn't working. Fix it! Fix it!" He released her and struck the board with doubled fists. Freed, Jessy nevertheless could do nothing but watch him beating at the board.

"They agree with me! They do! They do! I'm the one who is right. Why don't they call?" He charged to his feet suddenly, the movement knocking Jessy almost to the floor. Then making an animal-like sound of rage, he bolted for the door, tore it open and flung his way outside, into the street.

Jessy caught the stool, pulled herself up and sagged against the switchboard. Was it finished? She bit her lip so hard she tasted blood. Was he gone, not to come back?

How long she sat in front of the board, motionless, Jessy had little idea. Later, she looked up. The telephone office door was being cautiously opened. A new spasm of trembling shook her. Then she saw that it was only Hannah Lewelling and her sister, Marvella. They stepped inside and looked about like a pair of worried owls. Each wielded a wicked-looking closed parasol. "Is he gone? Are you alone, Central?"

Jessy could laugh, weakly. "I'm alone."

"We came to help you," Marvella said. "We think the mayor's lost his mind, poor soul."

Hannah looked thoughtful as she added, "Central, we're glad you spoke out today. We want you to know we're with you, and Cecil and little Anna Cora. It's time somebody finally spoke out against what's gone on here. We are all God's people, after all. Just being kind to one another would do so much for this world."

Jessy nodded. "Thank you."

"Does this mean you're staying in Ardensville, Central?" Marvella wanted to know. "We need you. You're a good member of our community, we're proud of you."

If she had walked away from the trouble here—added to the Farley thing—she would have hated herself forever, Jessy realized suddenly. She was about to reply to Marvella's question when Etta Moorehouse dashed into the telephone office. "You're all right! Oh, Jessamyn, I was so afraid for you. I just came from Mandy's. She told me what you did. Thanks be to God you weren't hurt. I came into town to wait for Tom and Hatch's train," she explained.

Jessy came off the stool in a hurry and caught Etta's hands. "Is Hatch—did he get in?"

"Any minute. The train's a little late. I left word for the agent to send Hatch over here the second he gets off the train."

She hadn't wanted him involved before, but oh, now it was all right.

Others came. As the room began to fill, Jessy apologized for not having enough chairs. No one had seen Hale. Where he had gone, no one knew. Jessy worried that Anna Cora and Cecil and Gussie didn't reach Lilli's.

She could scarcely believe her eyes when Lilli herself slipped through the telephone office door. "Anna Cora and Cecil and Gussie Stuberg are okay at my place," she called across the room, in answer to Jessy's worried face. "Bill doesn't know I'm gone, but I had to come to you, kid."

The girls went into each other's arms, laughing and crying at the same time. Jessy saw that there was color in her friend's face, different from the last time she'd seen her, and there was a light in her eyes. "You look good, Lilli!" Jessy exclaimed, pulling back.

"You did it. What you did today! Annie and Cecil and Bill and Gussie told me everything. Oh, kid, on your own, you did it, Jessy. The morning glory opened up."

"Better late than never," Jessy said with a smile.

Townspeople still crowded into the telephone office, all talking at once. Word of what had happened had spread, even to those without telephones. Lucian and his little brood came. Jessy kept an eye out for Hatch, but so far, he hadn't come. She took Lilli aside. "Are you sure Cecil and Anna Cora will be all right? I'm so afraid of what Lombard Hale might do. He went running out of here so—I don't know—like he was—"

"Really wiggy," Lilli stated. "They say his speech sounded the same way." Her expression changed to a delighted grin. "Hold onto your hat, kid, I see a cowboy charging up the street like a ferocious bull." She nodded toward the plate glass window.

"Hatch!" Jessy ran. In another minute, he was inside, and she was in his arms. "Oh, Hatch," she sobbed brokenly against his warm shirt front, "I almost left—I almost lost you." His arms tightened about her.

"Oh, honey, the chance you took, and me not here," he whispered against her hair. He smothered her face with endless warm kisses.

Soft exclamations from their audience brought color to Jessy's cheeks. "Hatch," she said, "we're not alone."

"Don't give a damn." His lips caught hers in a firm, lingering kiss."

"Hate to break it up," Lilli said, clearing her throat, "but here's more company, Jessy."

It was the county sheriff. "Got your call, Central," he said, making his way through the crowd to Jessy. "I'm ready to go pick up this gent, but I'm shorthanded today. Saw this bunch in here and thought I'd get some help." He looked at Hatch, then at Tom Moorehouse who had come puffing in a minute or two after Hatch. "Want to come?"

"Sure do," Hatch agreed. "C'mon, Tom, this time let's get something done about this fella."

Jessy let go of him reluctantly. "Be careful, Hatch, please?"

"I ain't the one in this family that keeps risking their neck." He grinned and kissed her cheek. "Don't go nowhere. I'm coming back to talk to you about that family part."

There was nothing to do but wait. Her visitors decided that with the sheriff in town taking over, they could go home. Over the next hour, they left in two's and three's, wishing Jessy well and still asking her to stay. "Thank you, Jessy," Lucian told her. With hands linked and chins high, he and Grandma, Chris, and the little girls, went home.

Lilli kept Jessy company until they saw Hatch coming back. Jessy ran to meet him. "Is everything all right? Did you find him?"

"We found him." Hatch shook his head, a sad, puzzled expression in his eyes. "He'd gone clean off his rocker. We found him just a settin' in his porch swing. Gentle and meek as a kitten, saying stuff but makin' no sense. He didn't give any trouble." Hatch looked at Lilli, "I run into your friend, Bill Washburn; he's looking for you, Lilli, scared to death something'd happened to you. I said you were all right, and I'd send you home."

"Better go, then," Lilli said.

"I wonder what's going to happen to Hale?" Jessy asked, and Lilli hesitated to hear Hatch's answer.

"The sheriff, the doc, and a gent from the drugstore named Pierce are taking him to the county mental hospital for now. Hale's little girl was there. She was sayin' something about her daddy wanting things just so. He was awful dissatisfied with himself because he wasn't able to keep his wife healthy and alive, or his daughter from being slow. Having a perfect town with his mother's name on it was the one thing he felt sure he could do."

Jessy was silent, thoughtful, touched with pity for Lombard Hale, even though he had wanted her dead. "And nobody else came and tried to stop you or anything?" she asked, thinking of the other members of the Klan, Hale's faithful followers. Hatch knew what she was asking. "Nobody. And that was a surprise, after all that's been going on in this town. But the guy from the drugstore said the Ku Klux Klan was beginning to fall apart here after that body was found at Oriel Creek."

Lilli commented, "The Klan might never have gotten started in Ardensville except for Hale being so against outsiders."

"Yes," Jessy agreed, "but I think most everybody realizes now that when Hale brought in the Klan, he marred the town he loved instead of helping it." That reminded her, "Lombard Hale didn't want a police department, but I think that's changed now. It's needed."

"When's my smart little girl goin' to shush so I can get a word in?" Hatch lamented. He gathered Jessy into his arms.

"Time for me to go," Lilli said. "But first, I want you two to know that Bill says he'll run for local police chief if folks want him. If he does, don't forget to vote! I want a working husband so I can spend my time writing." She winked. "Invite us to your wedding, and we'll invite you to ours." She ducked out the door.

"Blasted girl stole my thunder," Hatch complained. His expression softened as he looked down at her. "Jessy, will you marry me? Will you do me the honor of being my wife?" Before she could answer his lips came down on hers. "Jessy, I love you so," he whispered.

A fine warm delight ran through Jessy. "I love you, too, Hatch. Yes, I'll marry you."

He kissed her nose, her eyebrows, her chin. "I aim to be a rancher someday, remember," Hatch said huskily, "an' I want a half-dozen or so kids. How do you feel about that, sweetheart?"

"The ranch? Or the kids?" She sighed. "Both sound good to me."

"Right away?" he asked softly against her hair. "We won't have to wait a fool year to be married, or any time like that, will we?"

Jessy's lips parted to say "right away," but a nagging thought that she'd left something undone stopped her. *Farley.* She couldn't bring him back, though. But was that what she'd wanted all this time, to have his death undone so she wouldn't have to face it? The hard feelings she'd held for his parents, did she *blame* them for Farley's existence? Did she blame them because they'd brought him into life and thereby made the tragedy happen? If that were true.... Deep shame filled Jessy.

Life wasn't ever going to be trouble-free, she could see that. And yet, for so long she had used up so much—of herself—trying to wish away what had happened. Blaming herself for something she hadn't done, yet not doing what she should have done. What a waste.

"Hatch," she said, "I have to go home, back to Seena, where my folks live, before we can get married. There are some people there I want to talk to, about something I should have had the sense to take care of long ago. I'll go right away. It won't take long. As soon as I get back, we'll be married."

Partly, she realized now, it was her own—*deceit* she couldn't or wouldn't face, letting Farley believe she loved him when she didn't—and losing his life thinking it was so. She pressed her tear-wet face against Hatch's chest. Knowing what love really was had helped so much—for her to grow, to see things better.

In her mind, Jessy could see herself going home to The Ranch, to Mama and Papa, to Willow and her new baby girl, to all her family. How dear they would always be. And what wonderful news she had to share with them. She hugged him tight.

Hatch!

Colophon

MORNING GLORY AFTERNOON was designed by Dennis and Linny Stovall of Blue Heron Publishing in collaboration with Larry Milam, the cover artist, and John Laursen of Press 22.

Type faces (digitally founded by Adobe) are Janson Text, set 11/14 for the body, and Caxton for titles and folios. All camera ready copy was digitally composed on a high resolution computerized imagesetter, with design, typesetting, and page layout done using Aldus PageMaker 4.01 on Apple Macintosh computers.

Janson was designed by Nicholas Kis in 1690, but was erroneously credited to Anton Janson, a Dutch printer.

Caxton is more recent. It was designed in 1981 for Letraset by Leslie Usherwood. In contrast to Janson, Caxton has short ascenders and descenders. Like Janson, it is predominantly a text face, though one that works well in display.